BROKEN EARTH

S.J. SANDERS

Broken Earth
Argurma Salvager Book 1
A Cybernetic Alien Romance

S.J. Sanders

A blue-green planet filled the viewscreen. Dawn was just breaking over the horizon and the planet's face was largely concealed in darkness, without the clusters of light that came with advanced civilization. Despite the aged fragments of satellites that orbited the planet, there was no indication from the ship's sensors that any of the indigenous civilizations remained, or that sentient life lingered after their fall.

All signs pointed to decay… and wealth for an enterprising salvager.

The sole occupant of the ship watched the viewscreen stoically as his vessel analyzed the information from the small probe ejected into the stratosphere. His cybernetics streamed the data directly from the core systems as he interpreted the transmissions, and data scrolled across his left visual receptor.

One long, pointed ear twitched, betraying his interest.

The chemical composition of the atmosphere was suitable for sustaining Argurma lifeforms, although the gravitational pull would be less intense than on Argurumal. His systems automatically calibrated for ideal mobility as he narrowed his eyes on the planet that grew larger at his approach. Scans detected valuable minerals and metals for optimal scavenging potential. The male trilled low in his throat with anticipation.

Turning from the viewscreen, Veral'monushava'skahalur commanded his chair into the pilot station. With a click in his throat, he issued a command that summoned his hunting dorashnal. Krono glided up on six paws, taking his place at Veral's feet. The dorashnal's glossy black scales reflected the low light from the viewscreen as the six prehensile vibrissae surrounding his head flared in a relaxed manner. One twined around Veral's hand as he patted the beast. Though there wasn't so much as a flicker in his flat expression, he felt a deep fondness for it. Despite knowing that such attachments were foolish, he was bonded with his dorashnal like every Argurma.

Since his adolescence, when he received the first of his cybernetic implants at the first sign of his sexual maturation, he'd had few attachments. His ship and his dorashnal, who had been his companion since they were pups together, were all that mattered in his world.

That and the driving desire to accumulate credits to see to his upgrades and needs.

Veral did not adhere to the illogical behavioral codes upheld by his race. Nor did he give any of his attention to the bonds of loyalty that so many felt toward their world. Such attachments exploited a weakness that he refused to possess, one that was fundamentally dangerous as far as he computed. He'd disabled that coding the moment he discovered it many solars ago. Even now, he regularly sent his nanocybernetics through his systems to look for any sign of the homeworld infiltrating his coding to renew their hold on him.

Veral'monushava'skahalur belonged no one.

Instead of serving as a warrior in the planetary armed forces or as an assassin hunter for the Council of Twelve, he'd devoted solars to establishing his reputation not only as a ruthless fighter but an unparalleled salvager among the Intergalactic Federation. Moments like these always brought him many credits from the contacts he'd made.

As Veral settled back into his seat and initiated the landing sequence, his glowing blue orbs narrowed with satisfaction. There were many who would give him great wealth for even a fraction of what he detected on the planet surface. It was a shame that his ship was not equipped to transport live animals. The life signs of numerous species made him curse his short-sightedness. The creatures would have been profitable.

He tapped one of his three thick, heavily scaled fingers on the console beside him as the planet steadily filled the viewscreen. His long, dark claw clicked a tempo on the metal as his systems targeted one of the crumbling cities in the interior of the landmass with low humidity. Argurumal was a planet of rolling sands, where water was contained in deep replenishing wells within the ground. He found planets with high water ratios to be disconcerting at best. He preferred to stay away from them when possible.

The ship rumbled and jerked as it dropped through the atmosphere, heat searing the sides of the vessel. The viewscreen was dark during this phase of descent, leaving him blind save for what the ship's monitors told him via his constant connection with them. Still, when at last the viewscreen snapped open, he couldn't resist a smile.

Descending among vivid rocky inclines of brilliant hues, Veral marveled at the topography of the region. The rising sun dyed the rocks impressive shades of orange and red, stretching out to great distances from all sides. Just ahead, he could see the sprawl of what must have once been a city.

Although he was tempted to land within the city for his convenience, experience had taught him the hard lesson of keeping his ship concealed outside of his work area. He didn't need any of the indigenous wildlife getting curious about his ship. Memories of the mandra swarm on SerHava that followed him to his ship each night, attacking with stingers and claws, served as a reminder. He wasn't interested in a repeat performance and, given how seriously they'd compromised his ship, he couldn't afford to take damage so far away from any outposts.

This part of the universe was an outlying area that few were willing to expend credits and fuel to explore. Sometimes pirates came into the Dark Zone to avoid detection and made it their home, but he doubted even pirates had been this far into this sector. They wouldn't waste their precious fuel crystals for anything outside of subverting intergalactic patrols—what little there were. As he began the landing sequence, he shook his head at the thought of how many delixar crystals he'd fed into his engine.

Not that it mattered now. It was too late to recalculate another route outside of the Dark Zone. He'd already traveled far beyond the marked boundaries, and this was the first salvageable planet he'd come across since entering. He had put a massive amount of his saved credits into stored fuel. If the trip wasn't as profitable as he'd hoped, he had plenty of fuel to explore several more planets before he would need to return to Federation space. Still, his calculations told him that he was on the mark for this planet.

With an ease that came from numerous landings, Veral directed his ship away from the gray metal and broken stone of the ruins as the landing systems engaged. The blocky, rough buildings looked more primitive than what he typically found in his line of work. He shifted his weight with the vessel as it rocked and settled on the uneven ground. The hiss of its landing gears decompressing sounded too loud in the silence of the navigation center. Locking his flight grid and all controls, Veral rose to his feet and descended to the lower level of his ship.

At his approach, the shell door hissed as it depressurized and slid up into its frame. A narrow metal platform immediately extended the short distance to reddish sand below. Fine grains scattered inside with a hot breeze, prompting him to close the thin membranes of his secondary lids to protect his eyes.

His eyes weren't the only thing assaulted. Veral's senses were overwhelmed by the scents of unfamiliar flora, decay, and the mineral bite of sun-warmed sand. His cybernetic memory banks cataloged everything he saw for analysis later as he made his first steps on the new world.

Aside from a large amount of rock and sand, small green plants clung stubbornly to life, not unlike the low, reddish shrubs of his home planet and yet their shape was unlike anything he'd seen. Bending down, he grabbed ahold of a small plant and gave it a hard yank, breaking free a small sprig that he slid into a sample vial.

A small, bright-colored creature with a long, thin tail scurried out from a rock in search of shelter elsewhere. He watched curiously as Krono darted out after the tiny animal.

The dorashnal's tail whipped around him as he sniffed the ground with interest and growled a series of rattling clicks. Veral stood once more to his full height and ignored the beast. Krono was often distracted by odd fauna, but he would alert him to a threat without delay. His processors observed another small animal—this time brown—scurrying over the sand seconds before Krono took off after it and promptly dismissed it. He did, however, make note of valuable food sources present as he proceeded toward the ruins.

The buildings, he discovered, although in early states of decay, were still functional enough to offer respite from the heat of the sun as it climbed higher in the sky. While many buildings had nothing more than metal skeletons remaining, he noted that the lower floors were often structurally intact to some degree. Many places had entire walls missing but seemed otherwise untouched, yet in lower, exposed openings, he could see where the sand was beginning to accumulate and drift further inside.

It seemed that no matter where he was, the desert was universally eager to devour everything from the most common to the sacrosanct.

One building he passed drew his attention, its colored glass set in its windows with images of odd, smooth beings staring serenely. He cocked his head and regarded it with silent calculation. It appeared quite different than the other buildings around it and it piqued his curiosity. Veral peered at the edges of the frame to see how he might be able to remove the glasswork. He knew a collector on his homeworld who would slaver over such rare art.

Argurmas had a love for glass and there were clans who specialized in glasswork. Alien glass samples of such quality would be highly prized. He had no doubt that many would flock to an offworld auction for an opportunity to acquire it.

As he scanned the glass, movement within the building caught his eye. Long-tailed insects possessing noticeable stingers scrambled over the rocks and sand inside the building. As he watched them crawl over the sand, he saw the flash of reflected light off the eyes of a small, dull-colored predator that crouched near an upturned slab of wood from the floor. He smiled grimly at them. He wanted to see more of the city before he started collecting, but he would be back even if the place was swarming with small predators.

If they attempted to bite him, they would soon discover that he bites back.

Veral continued examining the buildings as he made his way down the road. Most of them were barren of anything except for primitive computing units and a small selection of furniture, if any at all. These did not appear to be dwellings but were likely once used for industry or socializing. While these places could, at times, prove profitable—such as in the case of the computing units which could be stripped down for metals—the easiest sources were always residential areas where sentient beings collected property. That was what he was searching for. Certainly not broken windows with ragged textiles and buildings yawning with wide, empty spaces. There was, however, a promising handful of places that seemed to have once sold primitive technology. He made note of each of them.

One particular shop had numerous mounted screens, and although they were cracked and damaged, he grinned in anticipation of pulling them apart. This trip was going to be far more profitable than he'd imagined! He was still smiling as he left, but his smile fell when his eyes landed on a strange fresh marking on the side of the building. Crouching down so that he was eye level with it, he ran a finger over it and lifted his hand up, rubbing his fingers together. The pigment was dry. No one had come upon him with him unaware of their presence and yet it still had the sharp scent of new pigment. The mark itself was odd and crude in appearance. *Perhaps it is from a species possessing enough intelligence to utilize low-tech weapons and tools.* That wasn't unusual to find among animals. All the same, he considered it prudent to be cautious from that point on.

Where Veral was vigilant, Krono seemed unconcerned. He'd long caught and consumed the furry animal and was investigating every crumbling alley for more prey. This prompted numerous little creatures that Veral surmised to be rodents to scurry out of their hiding places in a manner that disgusted him. After the third time, he impatiently summoned Krono to his side as they ventured farther into the heart of the city. Krono kept an eager pace, and Veral's exploration remained uneventful despite his unease. As the day wore on, he felt increasing discomfort until the moment he entered a residential zone and breathed in the astringent flavor of woodsmoke on the air.

Veral stopped in the middle of the road, his head turning as he attempted to pinpoint the direction it was coming from. The smell of salted fat left out in the sun also scented the air beneath the odor of smoke. Its foul perfume turned his stomach. While he'd been able to dismiss the markings as something created without logical reason by primitive beings, the scent of fire, grease, and burning flesh ran contrary to his original hypothesis.

These were the lingering remnants of what he'd assumed to be an extinct species. Not that they were likely to last long before those remaining few died out. The probability of the indigenous species posing any possible threat to him was so minimal that it was almost amusing to entertain thoughts of a rogue assault against him.

He looked around, but when no threat made itself known, Veral retrieved a disc from his belt and placed it on the ground to activate it. The disc wobbled and then erupted into metal pieces that folded out until they slid together and formed a basic salvage collector cart. He took a step and watched as it followed behind him as it was designed to do. Most beings had to get implants, but he merely updated his processors to include the lure codes for the device. Satisfied that the cart was working properly, he plundered the first houses he came across. He stripped salvageable electronic parts for their metals, retrieving a few gems from dust-lined containers that he pulled out from the grimy wooden cubes with little effort. His nasal ridges immediately pinched to protect his sensitive olfactory cavity from any spores that may rise into the air with the dust motes that billowed around him.

As the afternoon wore on, Veral accumulated scrap at a satisfyingly regular pace. After the second dwelling, he found it necessary to deploy another collector cart. Both trailed behind him as he progressed through the residential district. There was little noise to distract him from his task other than the sounds of small animals running for cover at his invasion into their space.

That was until the sound of a small engine caught his attention. Veral paused to listen to it. His processors worked in an attempt to identify the sound and narrow down its direction. He chuckled to himself when he realized what it was. He was hardly concerned with who might be piloting it—they were no match for him. Instead, he was elated at the unmistakable sound of a small engine.

A primitive working engine could be highly profitable. It sounded rough and unstable, but that mattered little to him. He did not want it for everyday use. Unfortunately, the noise receded before he could get a lock on it. Veral's mouth twisted into a frown, his good humor evaporating as the object of his interest eluded him.

His vibrissae buzzed around him with irritation as he stepped around a building, the short mandibles of his jaw distorting to reflect his ill humor. He turned his head to call Krono when a smooth club struck him on the side of his head. White light shot through his vision and he roared, the sound nearly drowned out by a terrified scream.

Veral spun around, his vibrissae whirling and snapping in a frenzy as he searched for his attacker. The dorashnal snarled and would have rushed forward to attack, but Veral stopped him with a single command.

He wanted to take this blood himself.

He felt a rush through his systems of unmistakable excitement for battle. His enemy wouldn't be much of a challenge, but he was curious what this planet had to offer.

A small pale alien like the one he'd seen in the glass faced him. It didn't have scales, vibrissae, or any manner of external protection except a long, useless mane of soft filaments. It looked up at him with wide eyes as it gripped an insignificant, smooth club in its hands, swinging it with a bravado that was almost admirable even though its pale blue irises were ringed with white in a manner that he suspected betrayed its terror. His chest expanded, his muscles stretching in a demonstration of his power. As anticipated, it backed away from him. He snarled threateningly down at it.

The small being shook their head and muttered a guttural series of words in their soft, lilting voice as they dropped their arms and scrambled back. His translators worked to adjust and connect it to one of the languages his vessel had picked up and decoded as it continued to speak under its breath. He decided to refrain from killing the fragile thing for the time being. Its language could be useful if he ran into any more of the species and found himself needing to question them. He waited and allowed it to put distance between them.

"…fuck this. No crumbling piece of shit house is worth getting myself killed for. Have at it, asshole."

He did not understand all the words, but he frowned all the same. He suspected the inferior creature was trying to insult him. Infuriated, he let out a bass bellow that made the alien cringe and flee. He considered giving chase, his blood ramped for the kill, but he was distracted by a series of long, mechanical bangs. Veral slipped through the shadows, heading for the source of the commotion. Sliding between the metallic remains of what he could only surmise had once been primitive land transports, Veral hissed and waited for his new prey to appear.

When they came into view, they appeared remarkably distinct from the alien that he'd seen before. Larger, rougher, and heavier in build, several beings were clustered on the back of a dull red vessel, its coloration badly peeling. Two of them made loud noises as they lifted long weapons in the air, firing projectiles. Veral curled his lip at the wastefulness as his processors tracked the moving transport and he activated his telescopic vision in his right eye to get a closer look at his quarry. Two were wiry, and the third was of thicker girth. All three had dirty filaments sprouting from their faces which did nothing to improve their overall appearance.

"Right! Go right, Frank!" the one leaning forward shouted at the one piloting the vessel. "I could swear I just saw her slip between those buildings over there!"

"Shut up, Mike. I can see just fine," the pilot retorted back, turning a circular steering device sharply.

Another gripped a protrusion between its legs and hooted.

"Hell yeah! We're going to get a sweet little cunt tonight!"

Veral wondered at the gesture as the vehicle bounced in their rapid approach. Argurma males kept their reproductive civix in that same place, but few species in the cosmos had similar reproductive systems. Even in the unlikelihood that their species shared this trait, it still didn't lend Veral any understanding to the gesture or enlighten him as to their purpose.

Not that it mattered. They were prey, and he was certain that they might have something of value upon them.

As the transport closed in on his location, he could scent them clearly. All three of them reeked of sour drink, sweat, and rotten food that seemed to be splattered on their coverings. They behaved more like beasts as far as Veral was concerned, more so as their volume seemed to increase as they closed in on their prey.

He would kill them swiftly so that he wouldn't be forced to touch them overly much. He didn't desire to clean their filth off of him.

His muscles tensed, springing forward as the transport roared by him, his cybernetic-reinforced claws dragging into the metal body of the vehicle. It jerked roughly against him, jolting to the side at the heavy impact of his body, but he clung tight to the frame, his ears and vibrissae flattening against his head.

"What in Sam Hill…?!" one of the aliens barked in surprise.

Digging claws deeper with every move, Veral dragged himself up the side of the transport. The sound of the engine was so loud that it blocked out his hearing almost entirely, but he did not let it concern him. He drew up behind one of them, his nasal cavity closing to assuage the terrible smell, and he lifted a hand to strike. The vehicle rocked as something struck the side dangerously close to his position. He whipped his head around and rattled threateningly as another transport crested a mound of refuse beside them. Lights mounted from the top of the vehicle flashed and were responded to by several others that roared up from all sides of him.

"Holy shit!" a gruff voice bellowed from the vehicle that fired upon him. "Frank! You've got a—I don't know what it is. You have something on your truck!"

Veral squinted as lights hit him, his pupils retracting into narrow bands. He flared his vibrissae, allowing them to rattle threateningly around him as he growled, baring his fangs and extending his sharp mandibles. The aliens on the transport with him shouted to each other and began to fire at him. A few projectiles glanced off him, but most didn't come close to hitting his shielding technology. Irritated, he lifted one of his blasters.

"Fuck me, it's armed! Take it out, boys! Phil, deploy the net! Don't look at me like that! We aren't going to catch that girl if this big bastard kills us all. Fire it!"

A large net shot over Veral with such force that it knocked him off the back of the transport and onto the ground. It was soon followed by several others. Despite their weight, he pushed himself to his feet, determined to destroy them all when booted feet surrounded him. Veral growled threateningly, promising them a painful death in the most intimate manner of his people when sharp spikes hit him, and electric currents swept through his body. His organic mind whited out even as his circuitry went offline.

2

In a dark corner of a crumbling building, two walls shy of anything remotely resembling suitable shelter, Terri hissed as she dug a ricocheted bullet out of her thigh. It was painfully obvious that the Red Reaper Gang was getting worse. She'd heard rumors that many of the local boys started joining up in droves soon after they arrived in Phoenix at the promise of plenty of food, moonshine, and women.

It was the latter that had Terri preparing to leave the city.

The gang was rounding up every woman in sight. Phoenix was a dangerous place for anyone female. It wasn't particularly healthy for the guys either. Not that anyone could tell any of them that with the way so many were flocking to the gang. Most of the men who had families were smart enough to leave when the rumors began. She should have left with them while she had the chance. Instead, she'd been among many of the women who had refused to be ousted from their homes.

At the time she had reasoned (as many women had) that they had survived all their lives living in a harsh world—how much worse could the gang make it? Her father objected strenuously but she'd refused to leave him. His body had become frail since he suffered a debilitating sickness, making him dependent on her for everything. With her mother dying years ago in childbirth, along with her baby brother, all they had was each other. She had stuck by him and laughed at any threat.

Now she had to admit that she had been very wrong.

Not for staying with her father—she refused to regret that—but for not taking the gang seriously. The Red Reapers were not just another nuisance but a living, breathing plague, infesting everything around them. They claimed women as their right. Any woman who didn't submit to them was hunted down like prey. It was bad enough that some women she'd known all her life, strong women as hard as standing rocks in the desert, willingly sought out the gang to be welcomed into their protection.

Terri snorted a dismal bark of laughter. *Protection?* Ha!

"Protection" meant that, instead of being hunted and passed around the members of the Reapers indiscriminately, she only had to please one master and anyone he might decide to share her with, if he shared at all. Or so she had been told by one of the women when she came across her foraging for food for the camp.

Terri refused to be one of them. A little more scavenging for food and water and she should be able to acquire enough to get her to the next settlement. Being injured would be a setback, however, although it could have been much worse.

She'd been lucky that catching a ricocheted bullet was all that happened. She'd come very close to being caught when that monstrous creature distracted her pursuers, prematurely pulling them from the hunt. She heard it roar and then their terrified shouts as she retreated. Although part of her wanted to go back and watch, she had beat a hasty retreat out of gratitude for her narrow escape. She would rather dig a bullet out any day.

Her blood ran cold as she remembered the men hooting and howling like wild beasts as they chased her in their attempt to herd her. They had been close on her heels when the sounds of chaos had erupted, among them a bellow of an enraged creature. Something inhuman, born from nightmares. She'd recognized it immediately. That terrible, rattling growl like death itself. It was when she paused to listen amid that distraction that she'd caught the stray bullet.

She clenched her jaw as the bullet slid out of her flesh, blood flowing freely as it emerged. Gritting her teeth, she doused the wound with the last bit of her alcohol, groaning with agony. Fuck, it burned!

"Son of a bitch," she panted as she wrapped her thigh tightly. She hoped there wouldn't be repeat occurrences. She was now out of alcohol, and while that seemed easy enough to replenish, medical gauze was getting harder to find.

She needed to get out of this hellhole. But she didn't think that the other cities fared much better. Chaos had erupted when the last wars destroyed their planet. It happened when her grandparents were young, and they told her stories of how life had been before the wars. Then, just like that, it was gone. Humanity turned on itself. Those who didn't die from airstrikes and biological weapons were picked off over the years by disease and the worst humanity had to offer: rape, murder... cannibalism.

Terri leaned back, her head falling against the wall, and stared at what had once been a family's living room. A faded portrait hung over a broken TV screen coated with dust, a smiling couple with two smiling kids and a baby. Infant toys still littered the living room from the family's final moments in their house. A broken Tonka truck was tilted on its side, forgotten by the little one who once loved it. A baby doll stared sightlessly nearby, its cheerful face broken, now a home for the insects that were skittering in and out of its cheek. Like many houses, it was a home of ghosts. The sooner she could get out of there, the better.

Her thoughts turned to the massive creature she'd encountered earlier. It most certainly had *not* been human and, given the technology it seemed to possess, she had little doubt as to what it must be even if her brain had difficulty accepting it.

An alien.

An actual, living, breathing alien had come to Earth when it was nothing more than a cesspit.

Terri closed her eyes at the irony of the situation. Humans had been so interested in contact with alien lifeforms when there had been something left of humanity to share. Then again, this alien didn't appear as if it were looking to communicate peacefully or share anything.

No, it had arrived among them like a jackal in the night, hunting for bones.

She shivered as her mind conjured its image. It was huge and sleek, every line of its body powerfully built with muscle like that of the jaguars that were occasionally seen on the outskirts of the city. There had been no empathy or pity in its glowing gaze, only raw, predatory interest. She'd been terrified and then thankful that its attention had been redirected to the gang members hunting her. She had no doubt that after her reactive assault, driven by her instinct to attack anyone who intruded uninvited on her hiding place, the alien would have happily torn her apart piece by piece for her daring. Certainly, it had sought to intimidate her.

What was there not to be intimidated by? The alien easily stood taller than seven feet, its entire body covered in dark silver scales. Large spikes curved out from the hip joints, shoulders, wrists, and elbows like some sort of natural armor, and the claws on its three fingers and thumb were terrifying. She hadn't gotten a good look at its face—the whip-like, rattling coils framing its head absorbing most of her attention—but she was surprised that what she had seen hadn't made her piss herself. Yet, other than intentionally scaring her, the alien hadn't made a move to hurt her. That had been kinder than anything her pursuers would have done.

Who was the true monster in that scenario?

Resting her cheek on her dirty jean-clad knee, she sighed, wondering what happened to the creature. The sounds of pain and anger rang through her mind. What had the gang done to it? She felt certain that they would find someone to torture it just for shits and giggles if nothing else. She'd watched in horror, helpless to intervene when several of the men set an elderly man on fire. They'd laughed when he ran terrified and in pain through the city center. They would have no trouble tearing apart an alien to satisfy some perverse amusement.

Shaking her head, she leaned over and pulled a dusty can out of her scavenging bag. She held it up to the light and sighed. The label had fallen off long before she found it but given the size of the can, it was unlikely to be fruit or vegetables. Those had been exhausted some time ago.

Oh well. Mystery meat was still food, and Terri wasn't one to turn her nose up at what scraps she could find.

Popping the pull tab, she peeled the tin lid off and sniffed the contents. Chicken. Plucking a bland chunk out of the can, she popped it in her mouth. She was grimacing at the rubbery taste when the sound of a plaintive whine made her halt mid-chew and glance around.

Was that a dog? She hadn't seen a dog in three years. As food became scarce, man's best friend moved to the top of the menu for many people. Terri squinted at the deep shadows of a wall that opened out into the street. Her breath caught and her belly twisted with nerves when nothing appeared. Was it a trick or a trap of some kind meant to lure someone out? She didn't move as she strained to listen. Her skin prickled when, again, she heard the loud whine.

"Who's there?" She whispered into the gaping darkness deep within the recesses of the falling-down building. Something large moved within the shadows at the sound of her voice and it took all her self-control not to bolt to her feet. The thudding of her heart echoed in her ears as she stared, her breath coming out in shaky gasps. The clear silhouette of a massive canine moved in the shadows. It darted by her, turning nervously before lying on its belly just out of sight. She slowly set her can down and leaned forward. Swallowing, she reminded herself that it was just a dog… Nothing to necessarily be afraid of. She liked dogs.

"Hey, baby. Come here," she called out, patting her leg. The dog turned its head toward her, and she could feel it watching her as it whined once more. Poor thing was probably afraid. She air-kissed and wiggled her fingers in encouragement. Its long ears tilted toward her and it bobbed its head in response, creeping forward on its belly as she continued to make kissy noises at it. She smiled with relief as it neared the sunlit room. A small thrill shot through her at the thought of finally having a companion again. She'd been alone for far longer than what was probably healthy. She was tired of it.

"Good baby," she crooned with excitement. She leaned forward as she attempted to get a good look at the breed. It was large—as in alarmingly, excessively large. She wondered if it was a Great Dane. She remembered the breed from books she had loved as a child. Her lips split into a wide smile as she scooted forward eagerly.

All good feelings fled from her when inky tendrils seemed to move around it in an eerie serpentine fashion. She could feel the blood receding from her face as she dropped her hand and began to scoot back. That… was not anatomically possible for a dog. As it stepped out of the shadows, she recoiled, flattening against the wall. Her heart pounded so violently in her chest that her entire world was filled with nothing but the sound of its furious beat.

That—that was definitely not a dog!

The shape of the creature was so similar to a canine that if she blurred her vision, she could almost retain the illusion and pretend that she wasn't looking at a creature that didn't belong anywhere on Earth. A shame that she'd never been good at self-deception. She wanted to know what was coming at her so kept her gaze focused on the animal approaching on—*holy fuck!*—six legs! Its paws scraped the ground as it continued to wiggle forward on its belly, sending small pebbles rolling with its forward momentum. It whimpered pitifully as she saw a face that had ridges and planes like a reptile and shiny black scales instead of fur. It had the same whip-like extensions around its head that the alien had. Though possessing some similarities, she suspected that it was some kind of companion or pet.

She exhaled in an attempt to ease her nerves. Two very long, pointed ears immediately tipped toward her and flattened as it whined again and crept forward at a quicker rate on its six legs. Terri would have backed up more if she'd had the room, but when its hindquarters came into view, she saw the double tail tucked nervously against its body. It was afraid and in pain. Down the sides of its flanks and haunches, the animal was streaked with blood.

She ached with sympathy. Poor, miserable thing.

"Nice pooch, good pup," she whispered.

The animal suddenly sprang up, scrambling the last several feet to her side so quickly that for a second time it nearly gave her heart failure. She drew back and yet she felt her fear drain away when it buried its flattened muzzle against the crook of her arm with a pitiful whine. Her fingers twitched as she looked down at it. It wasn't attacking her or even trying to grip her arm within its dangerously wide jaws. Instead, it let out a gusty sigh and settled into the comfort of her arms. Hesitantly, she lifted her hand. It really was ugly, like some sort of nightmarish hellhound. She wasn't sure if she even wanted to touch it. It lifted its strange pearl-colored eyes and stared up at her. That was pretty creepy, but she melted a little bit as it stared up at her wistfully.

"You poor, ugly thing," Terri whispered with a small smile as she proceeded to stroke the animal's head and neck. She flinched when its "hair" wrapped briefly around her fingers and wrist, though the wet glide of its tongue on her opposite hand eased her anxiety. Both of its tails thumped with pleasure, and a giggle burst out of her. The animal jerked its head up nervously as it eyed her. She kept her smile firmly fixed on her face as she flattened her hand gently against the side of its neck. Finally, it sighed and dropped its head into her lap once more. She moved her hand to stroke more of its neck and peculiarly rough ears. The textures were wrong but the happy rumble from the animal had her doubling her efforts as she scratched its scales.

It was alien, but as far as she could judge it was still a dog. She could handle that.

She not only liked dogs but trusted animals in this crazy world more than she trusted other humans. She stroked down, grazing over its ridged shoulders and chest. It jerked under her touch and she turned her head to get a better look at the area just behind its shoulder blades. She pulled her hands back as she stared down at the taser burns marring huge patches of skin on its lower torso. The Reapers had rounded up the few remaining generators from the ruins of the offices and schools that littered the city. They were the only ones in the city capable of charging anything. She had no doubt that the wounds were from a Reaper's taser.

She winced at the burns. She didn't have anything to treat them. The best she could do was rinse the area clean. Taking the little water left in her currently opened bottle, she poured it over its wounds. Water was precious in the desert, especially now, but she wanted to get a good idea of what she was dealing with. Gently, she wetted the entire stretch of its lower torso, dabbing at it with a cloth she recently washed. After several minutes of careful work, she was able to see the damage inflicted by the Reapers. Aside from the burns, it had lost several scales, leaving the exposed flesh angry and raw where it was split. Other areas were crusted with dried blood from where bullets apparently had grazed it, ripping off scales and leaving furrows in its hide that had already stopped bleeding.

Satisfied that it was at least clean, she leaned back against the wall and poured some water into her cupped hand, offering it. She didn't have a bowl and the water already trickled out of her hand, but its long gray tongue lashed out to greedily lick at every drop. She repeated the process until the bottle was empty. Bringing her hand back to its head, she leisurely stroked between its long ears.

"I'll find you a bowl tomorrow when I refill my water bottles at the spring. It's too dangerous to stay near water around here," she mumbled. "Though I have no doubt that you'll protect me, won't you?"

The animal lifted its head, regarding her intelligently before huffing at her and snuggling closer. She wasn't sure if that was an affirmation or amusement from her new friend, but she decided to be optimistic enough to go with the former interpretation. It was possible that she was assigning too much intelligence to a creature that may not have any more reasoning ability than a Golden Retriever, but somehow, she didn't think so. From the way that it looked at her, it had a lot more going on behind its strange eyes. She needed to believe that it would willingly protect her.

It had been a long time since she felt even remotely safe. Not since her father died trying to hide her from a Reaper raid when a routine that they'd done hundreds of times since the arrival of the gang went terribly wrong.

Terri blinked back tears and pushed back the memory as she smiled down at the beast.

"I guess every girl around here would be a lot safer if they had a monster like you to protect them," she said. "You're a very good beast to have around. I don't mind sharing my food, water, and fire with you. It isn't so scary with you here. You look bigger and meaner than the men around here, which is a plus in my book," Terri observed as she lightly rubbed its chest. "If you're a woman here, you can't trust males."

The beast gave an unnerving rattling, clicking sound and rolled on her lap as he bumped her hand to scratch at his belly, giving her an eyeful in the process. She choked back a laugh. "Sorry. Unless I'm wrong and males and females are built differently where you're from, you would have to be the one male exception to the rule. Right now, I can't think of anyone else I would trust my safety with."

He raised his head and chirp-clicked at her in agreement. That was going to take some getting used to. She looked down at him in quiet contemplation as she rubbed the alien's chest, neck and head once more until she was stroking her fingers over the scale between his eyes. They half-closed in pleasure at her touch, making her smile. Even the thin, rope-like tentacles around his head rippled sedately. Despite how unusual he was, this was… nice.

Pulling her hand away, she reached into her sack and opened

another can. The sound brought his head up to investigate, the
tentacles rattling in a quiet shushing sound as he watched her curiously, his nostrils expanding to sniff at the can. He chirped again
and Terri laughed. The bizarre hellhound had already charmed her.
With a grin, she set the can in front of him and watched him attack
it with gusto as she continued to stroke his thick neck.

It almost felt like he was sent to her to be hers, and hers alone.

Her smile fell. She couldn't ignore the fact that he wasn't hers.
He belonged to a very scary fucking alien, and no doubt desired to
be reunited with it. The thought didn't make her happy, although
she couldn't blame him. If she had anyone that cared about her
who was mean and terrifying enough to keep the Reapers at bay,
she wouldn't rest until she was reunited with them either. She gave
her companion a longing look. It was always possible that the alien
was dead…

Terri grimaced at the selfish direction of her thoughts. Despite
the world being utter shit, she had always prided herself on being
reasonably compassionate, sometimes more than was wise. She
sighed with self-loathing.

"I bet your big alien misses you too," she murmured in disgust.
"You're pretty incredible. The perfect companion for something big
and scary. I hope it terrorizes those assholes plenty before it comes
looking for you."

Her eyes slid closed, but she continued to stroke her new
friend.

"It's been a long time since I've had a dog," she said. "I wonder
if your master may not miss you too much and let me keep you. No
one would fuck with a woman who had you nearby." She laughed.
"You and your master are both scary motherfuckers. Crazy scary,
in fact. You do look like a Bedlam to me. I think I'll call you that."

Groaning, she leaned back once more and stared at the midday
light scattered across the room from the remaining broken glass in
the window. *Broken.* That pretty much summed up everything on
Earth. The entire planet was broken. The only good news was that
nature was recovering and starting to take over. In just a few

decades, humankind would probably be nothing more than a memory on the face of a world that they had no shame in destroying.

Scooting down, she lay her head on her pack and closed her eyes. She felt the alien shift its weight to settle next to her, his nose buried against her neck. For now, they would rest and recover. Everything else could wait.

3

*V*eral groaned as his processors rebooted and his mind swam back into consciousness. His mandibles opened and closed, tiny receptors on the thin inner membrane tasting the air. The foul taste of sewage, sweat, smoke, and spoiled meat flooded his mouth. He wrinkled his nose and attempted to move his head, only to perceive that he was restrained with something unfamiliar flooding his system, inhibiting his nanos and keeping him in a weakened state. He growled and strained, testing his restraints.

"Ah, finally you're awake," a raspy voice intruded. Veral's processors picked up on the native tongue and he turned his attention to the speaker. Another one of the filthy filament-faced beings. He sneered distastefully. He preferred the first one he saw. At least that one faced him respectfully in combat and hadn't been so... dirty. With this one, he felt nothing but disgust and a desire to rip out the eyes of the being looking at him as if *he* were a commodity.

He extended his mandibles and growled from deep within his chest. The alien paled and swallowed before it bared its teeth at him in a weak gesture. *Pathetic.* Veral rolled his eyes away from the being, uninterested in giving it any more of his time. He would close his eyes altogether, but he did not trust anything enough to willingly close his eyes around them. He didn't even sleep near others of his own bloodline since becoming an adult. Even litter-mates become potentially dangerous rivals.

To his frustration, the alien leisurely paced into his line of sight once more. It smirked as it looked at him while sucking on a stick that stank like jibwa weeds, a rank plant used medicinally only by the desperate. The alien cocked its head.

"I have to admit you're a fascinating creature. Ugly as sin, but terrifying… strong too, from what my men tell me. Right now, you're looking at me as if you wanna rip my innards out. I imagine you understand every word I'm saying too, don't you?" Its face wrinkled as it bared its teeth again with more enthusiasm.

Veral wasn't impressed. The teeth were dull and flat, and the jaws small and delicate in appearance. It was nothing compared to the massive jaws, mandibles, and sharp teeth of an Argurma. He bared his own teeth at it but the creature, although it stank and tasted of fear, had the audacity to laugh. Veral bared his own teeth in a terrible grin, threatening violence that was sure to come as soon as he regained complete control of his limbs and systems. He was gratified to see it stumble back a few steps.

The alien pursed its lips and let out a low, piercing sound. "You're something special, indeed. That's why, instead of just outright killing you for coming into our territory, I'm going to make you an offer." The creature paused as Veral snarled at the insult. "I'm sure you know that you don't have control. We're using our generators to shock your system in combination with some pretty powerful drugs. It took some experimenting to find a dosage that kept you unconscious. You're only awake now because I allow it."

"And what are you?" Veral growled back in a rough voice.

"I'm the only human being on this miserable planet you need to worry about. I am Marcus, President of these here Red Reapers. I run this place. Anything that goes on here does so only with my say so. Which brings me to the purpose of our little meeting. It has been reported to me that you're collecting various bits of junk. Old tech and metal mostly. We have no use for it, as you can imagine. We've already collected what we need and run off our own limited power systems. As far as I'm concerned, you can take as much of it as you like from the city with my blessing. All you have to do is one very small, insignificant thing for me in return. Do this and you'll be left in peace to work."

Veral narrowed his eyes on the human as he saved the species identification to his memory. His processors were already reporting wide-scale interference and damage. Despite the intentions of the technicians, they have never been able to create an invincible model when it came time for the change. Adult Argurmas were superior to other beings but could be damaged and overpowered, especially those who were far from the network of their planetary alliance. The worst of the damage to his systems would take months before his nanos would be able to repair it all and return him to optimal performance.

Although he wanted nothing more than to make the human suffer, he had to acknowledge that the offer was a good one and worth considering if it allowed him to carry out his work undisturbed. His salvaging was his primary concern, and he already lost a day. Still, logic demanded that he proceed with caution. Despite the numerous advantages to the proposition, he didn't trust this so-called president.

"What do you want?" Veral hissed, his body jerking as he felt another low-level jolt of energy shock his circuits.

"Really, it's a small thing," Marcus said as his lips twisted upward. He turned and gestured to another by a canvas structure. The human standing there nodded once and disappeared inside only to return minutes later hauling a smaller human with a smooth face.

"All right, I'm coming. Jeez, Dale," the smaller human snapped. Although it was not the same one he saw earlier, it had similar features and a pleasant pitch to its voice. "I'd better not be putting out to fuck another guy. You agreed I wouldn't have to do that anymore," it said.

Veral recoiled at the idea of anything touching him intimately. Unmated

Argurma did not possess sexual desire. It was an essential part of their programming that kept their people in line socially and limited reproduction. Unauthorized reproduction, especially across species, was a punishable offense on Argurumal. He snarled in objection but was ignored by the humans, much to his displeasure.

"Shut it, Meg," the one named Dale grumbled as it dragged the smaller one to Marcus's side. "Do what you're told and be thankful I'm not making you do worse."

Marcus smiled down at the small human and stroked a hand through the long dark filaments on Meg's head. If it had been Argurma, the vibrissae would have either attacked the offending touch or twined around it affectionately as one mated. A mate or parent was the only one who ever touched another's vibrissae. The long filaments on the human's head did not react, although it winced and flinched away from the touch.

"Relax, Meg," Marcus crooned. "You won't be required to fuck anyone right now. You're here as an example only."

Meg shook nervously, its wide eyes falling on Veral fearfully as Marcus turned it fully to face him. Marcus gestured the length of the human's body with one hand.

"My request is simple: I want you to hunt for me. I want more of these for my men. Women are prized commodities these days. They break too easy and are hard to replace. Their families hide them, and they make every effort to evade us despite the fact that we offer them protection in a cruel world. Isn't that right, Meg?"

Meg shied away from Marcus's touch but nodded in affirmation. "Yes, that is right. We're protected," the small human whimpered as the hand knotted tightly in its head filaments.

Veral watched, unmoved by the interaction, before finally grunting, unclear of exactly what the humans were talking about. Man and woman didn't translate in a way that he understood. "Why do you want women?" he asked at last.

Marcus watched him for a moment before bursting out into

laughter. "Surely our species work similarly in at least one fashion. Don't your males want females?"

Female. So that was it. Marcus and the other rough faces were males. Meg and the one from before were females. The males wished for him to procure mates for them rather than win them by their own efforts. Disdain rose sharply in his belly. He did not hold with the ethical code upheld by his species, but the rules of courting were sensible and for the wellbeing of everyone. The most that was permitted for an Argurma was to run their mate down and lock themselves together in a mating hold until the other yielded. They did not trap mates... and certainly not for other males. A male who wished a female had to conquer her on his own.

"You wish for me to gather mates for you," he snarled in offense.

Marcus lifted his shoulders carelessly. He didn't understand the gesture but read the expression on the male's face clearly. Callous disinterest.

"I wouldn't go so far as to say mates." He laughed with a contemptuous glance at Meg, who shrank before him. The sound was echoed by the other male, Dale, standing just behind him. "More like a pleasant diversion."

"We do have a few who are pregnant," Dale said with a chuckle.

"Unfortunately, not everyone in the camp is good at following directions," Marcus agreed with a sigh. "The bottom line is that we need enough women to keep the boys from trying to kill each other. Not enough pussy to go around makes them irritable. What I want is for you to hunt them out for us. We get women, and you get access to anything you want. What do you say?"

Veral sneered at the humans and turned his head away in disgust, allowing his silence to answer for him. He could kill and hunt at his leisure whatever prey he set his mind on. He even thought to hunt down the alien, the female, when he first saw her, but he would not help these lesser beings trap the female who remained in his thoughts for a dishonorable purpose. He would rather hunt her and subdue her, triumphant in his own victory over her strength, and kill her if necessary than turn her over to them.

"Very well," Marcus said at length. "Maybe we need to give you some time to think about it. Dale…"

A stream of energy lit through him with such strength that, though it had been brief, it was enough to disorient him. He watched through unfocused eyes and curled his lip as the human approached with a syringe. His body jerked as it was plunged into his neck, the drug pulling him down into darkness as his nanos remained disabled and helpless to aide him.

When he woke again, the sky was dark, the camp lit only by a fire in the distance. He inhaled, his mandibles flaring, and he caught the taste and stench of males near him. Furious, he opened his eyes. Several males were gathered around them. Many of them had their clothing opened, their strange, shapeless civix clenched in their hands as they stood near the fire. Several females had been brought out and were being held against the ground as the males took turns rutting into them.

Sex, aggression, and impatience flavored the air with its rank musk.

A male stepped away, his civix still leaking seed, revealing the female's oddly exposed wet quin as she shivered and made small noises in her throat. The glimpse was brief as another male slid behind her and thrust within the welcoming opening. She squealed beneath him, her hips jerking as the male pounded into her, his breath coming in grunts of pleasure. The display was both informative and disturbing, the way they shared a female together that clearly none were mated to.

His gaze shifted to several of the males who were peering at him curiously as they waited for their turn. One nodded to him as he spoke to the other by his side. "What do you think? Might be interesting to try and fuck that." He rubbed his civix as he eyed Veral.

"Dude, don't be stupid." His companion laughed. "It's an alien. It'll probably tear your junk off if you tried to stick it in anywhere."

Veral growled and rattled his mandibles aggressively in agreement. Just let any one of them attempt to get near him with their civix... He bunched his muscles, rattling the chains as he twisted violently. The males scurried away, stinking of terror. Its taste was to his satisfaction. He hissed, daring them to return. He didn't see the needle come toward him until he felt the wave of nothingness flood his veins, dragging him once again deep into his mind.

erri stepped gingerly around the rocks surrounding the spring. Even after a full day of rest, her leg still ached like a bitch. She stopped, balancing her weight on her good leg as she squinted through the harsh sunlight at her companion. Bedlam paced easily around her, his burns and minor injuries almost completely healed. The tiny tentacle "whips" didn't seem to move at all when he jogged close by her side, and they lay flat now as he watched her expressionlessly from where he was perched on top of a large rock. He didn't pant like a dog would in such heat. Between the glittering darkness of his scales, pearly eyes, and his sharp face that almost resembled a jackal if not for the massive hyena-like jaws, he resembled some sort of eccentric art born from a deranged mind more than a living animal.

Turning away from him, she squinted down at the spring, her dry tongue running over parched lips. The water trickled out in a small stream. It would take some time to fill her bottles, but the water flowed out from the limestone pure and clean. It was the safest place to get water in the entire city. She knelt down and scooped water into her mouth.

When she finally drank her fill, she sat back and peered up at Bedlam again to find him stretched out on the rock patiently. He was definitely well-trained. He had to be thirsty as well, but he hadn't bolted for the water. He didn't even seem to be looking at it. His attention was noticeably divided between her and the landscape.

"Come on. Bedlam. Come get a drink, boy," she said.

His ears perked her way and he glanced down. After a long, languorous stretch, he dropped down from the rock in a graceful bound. His little tentacles began to writhe toward her the moment he neared, his massive head and body brushing against her with affection. Terri laughed and patted his shoulder while she disentangled herself from the thin members grabbing onto her. Giving his shoulder a final pat and a light shove, she walked over to crouch by the trickling water. It puddled in a rocky dip at the bottom, at which Terri gestured.

"Go ahead. Get a drink while I fill this up," she said as she lifted up the metal canisters. Although they heated the water, she preferred them to the plastic bottles that left the water tasting strange after a while.

Bedlam sank down on his haunches, his long tongue snaking out to lap at the small pool of water. She watched for a moment— because it really was an absurdly long tongue—and notched the mouth of the bottle just below the natural spigot in the stone. Bedlam drank little water compared to what she was expecting for his size, and before she had even filled her first bottle, he jumped back onto the rock beside the spring, stretching out beneath the rays of the sun.

She was really curious about whatever world he came from that he could survive the heat and thrive with so little water. As if sensing her eyes on him, he turned his head to look back down at her, his long ears tilting toward her as he held her firmly in his regard before glancing away once more.

Terri laughed as she grinned up at him. It seemed that Bedlam was once again patiently waiting on her. He never seemed to completely relax, not even to doze in the warm rays of the sun. Even lying down as he was, his every sense seemed to be scanning the environment around them in a way that he hadn't done in the shelter. It occurred to her that he was more on edge since they were out in the open. The spring didn't have any buildings close by to provide cover if necessary. Just large rocks. It had never bothered her until now. Until watching him stare fixedly at one direction or another, his ears shifting at every sound, as if there were something out there beyond her ability to see. She hunkered down more at the side of the spring, feeling exposed, a shiver running up her spine.

It was almost worse that, every now and then, he lifted his head and gazed in the direction of the Reaper camp, as if foretelling of danger coming from that direction. That she was well aware of. Nothing good ever came from going near the camp. A smart woman wouldn't be so stupid to venture close nor to linger where they might find her.

Glancing up at the sun, she pursed her lips thoughtfully. The hour was still early enough that she suspected the entire camp was still sleeping off whatever brew they had concocted. The women would soon be out to look for food and water long before the men would wake. That was her only opportunity to learn what was going on beyond the walls. Her safety often depended on it. If she were fortunate, she would be able to meet with her contact and be gone long before anyone else arrived to gather water.

She was on her third and final bottle when Bedlam, sprawled out on the rock beside her, began to shake his whips around his head, creating a hissing rattle. He stiffly rose to his feet, his lip curled back from his sharp teeth as he stared ahead. Terri felt her neck prickle and slowly turned. Blood pounding in her ears, she was sure that she was going to turn and find one of the Reapers approaching. Her breath left her in a gust of relief as she instead saw the familiar face of her childhood friend.

"For fuck's sake, Meg," she breathed around a shaky laugh. "You scared me there. I thought for sure you were one of the Reapers." She peered at her friend's pallid face with concern.

"What's wrong with you? Did one of those bastards do something…?"

Meg swallowed noticeably, her eyes fixed on the spot just over Terri's shoulder. "What the fuck is that thing, Terri?" she whispered hoarsely.

Terri glanced behind her and winced as she saw Bedlam still standing menacingly over her. Though he had dialed it back a bit and was no longer baring his teeth, he was still very much on alert, looking like death incarnate. Turning back to her friend, she capped her bottle and stuck it in her back before lifting a hand in a calming gesture.

"No reason to be afraid. That's just Bedlam. I found him… Well, he found me, and we've been taking care of each other. He's some sort of dog, I think," she said, her voice trailing off as her friend's stare transferred to her.

"That's *not* a dog," Meg protested as she shook her head from side to side. "That's a monster, just like the thing the guys are keeping captured in the camp. It scares me to death, Terri. I swear, the look in its eyes—it looks at us as if it would kill everyone and not feel even the slightest bit of discomfort or remorse. You can't trust these… things."

That answered her question about what happened to the alien. If it was as bad as Meg said, perhaps it would be better just to leave it and let things work out on their own. She could keep Bedlam at her side and pretend that she never knew that the alien survived.

Her eyes trailed over Bedlam and she felt a surge of guilt for considering it. If she was going to let someone die in cold blood, she had to at least acknowledge what she was doing. Despite Meg's fear, Bedlam wasn't evil. She doubted that the alien deserved such a fate and completely lacked good qualities. Groaning, she rubbed her face with one hand and shoved it through her hair.

An idea took root in her mind as she looked at Bedlam. She was overlooking one huge benefit to helping the alien, one that made her almost breathless with excitement. It didn't just arrive by foot out of nowhere. It was an alien! It likely had a spaceship nearby and could fly from any place on the planet to another. A grateful alien *might* be willing to transport her… say …to the coast. She would be far from the Reapers and could cross the continually expanding desert safely—which itself was a terrible feat.

All she would have to do is sneak into the encampment and break it out. How hard could it be if she secured inside help and attacked when the men were guaranteed to be blitzed out on drugs and drink? She would suffer only minimal risk, especially considering that as soon as the alien was free, it would probably rip through anyone who tried to stop them.

She licked her lips in anticipation and smiled at her friend. It was an insane plan. There was no guarantee that the alien wouldn't outright kill her the moment she freed it. But what was the alternative? Hang around Phoenix and hope to scavenge enough before the Red Reaper boys caught up to her? Terri had already come to the conclusion that she was living solely on the grace of borrowed time. She didn't have much to lose.

When it came right down to it, she would trust her chances better with a scary-ass alien.

Inching forward, her smile widened. "Meg," she whispered, "I need you to do me a big favor and help me sneak inside."

Meg narrowed her eyes suspiciously. "Why would you want to do a stupid thing like that, Terri? You said you won't accept their protection. Why go inside?"

"I want to free the alien," she answered honestly.

Her friend snorted and stomped away a short distance before rounding on her. "That's fucking insane, Terri. I should have guessed you would say something like that with how you're cozying up to its pet," she hissed. "That thing will kill you!"

"If it does, so what?" Terri returned hotly. "I don't want to die, but if I don't find a way out of here before the Reapers catch me, I'm well on my way to dying in one form or another… We both know it. I can't hide for much longer, and what they would do to me would be worse than death. I would long for death until I finally managed to take my life to escape them. If I have to risk being killed by this alien for even the chance of escaping this hell-hole, I will!"

Meg stared at her incredulously for a long moment before her shoulders slumped and she sighed miserably. "Okay. I'm going on record to say that I don't like this at all, *but* I will at least feel better with it out of the camp. For better or worse, it's my home and I don't feel safe there since they brought it in." She met Terri's eyes sadly. "I wish that you would change your mind and submit your-self for protection. It isn't so bad when you're there willingly. You might even get a decent guy who doesn't share you too much with the others. I mean, sometimes it happens because there just aren't enough women to keep the peace, but you would be safe."

Turning away from her friend, she sought out Bedlam and found comfort in his solid presence before she trusted herself to speak.

"No," she replied at last as she struggled to keep her voice even. "I wouldn't be safe by any stretch of the imagination… no more than you are, even if you've convinced yourself otherwise. I love you, Meg, but I can't live like you do. I would be reduced to some-one's property, spending the rest of my life serving another's whim and slaking their desires. I can't do that. I won't. I'll take my chance with the alien." She turned and gripped her friend's hand urgently, desperate hope swelling within her as she spoke in a hushed voice. "You could come with me, though. We could escape to the coast together like we talked about before the Reapers came."

Meg stared at her and smiled wistfully as she gently pulled away. "I can't do that, Terri. I can't leave Dale. He's a bit of an asshole, but he cares about me. I don't want to go back to strug-gling to survive alone. But I will get you in, and we will both have what we want. Meet me late tonight by the gates. You shouldn't have too much trouble finding it. I can't do more than that without risking punishment."

"I understand," Terri replied. She winced as she heard Bedlam growl behind her. She thought he was growling at Meg, but her friend turned and glanced over her shoulder. When Meg turned back again, it was with a sense of urgency.

"Get out of here, Terri," she hissed. "One of the guys is coming down with some of the other girls. You don't want them to see you."

Terri nodded and slipped on her pack. "Thanks, Meg."

Her friend nodded with a watery smile and turned her back to her as she hurried to pull out her own water bottles beside the spring while Terri slipped around the rocks heading the opposite direction. Bedlam slid off the rocks like a shadow as he skirted around her, his whips twisting around him in agitation.

She didn't speak to her silent companion even after they had put a safe amount of distance between them and the spring. It wasn't like he could offer any words to comfort her. That he loped by her side was enough. There was no reason to fill the space with words for no one other than herself. Instead, she made her way through the broken city, scouting for food as she bided her time. She gathered random supplies and cracked open cans, sharing the contents with Bedlam as she kept a continuous watch on the slow drag of the sun across the heavens.

5

*T*erri cursed her own stupidity as she crept closer to the camp. Torches flared around the perimeter wall, ghost-lighting skulls and the impaled remains of people who attempted to resist the Reapers' encroachment through the city. It was a grisly sight even in the light of day, but at night it seemed to contain a dark malevolence that made her want to run in the other direction. The nearest head, freshly spiked, stared at her with sightless eyes, his mouth gaping open at her as if he were laughing. Bedlam sniffed at it until she snapped her fingers and patted her leg, drawing his attention away from it. His interest in the corpse made her want to gag.

Peering through the darkness, she relaxed as she made out the silhouette of her friend waiting for her. Meg stood just inside the entrance, a shawl clutched around her shoulders. The moment she spotted her, Meg frantically waved Terri in.

Terri ducked down along the side wall and hurried toward the entrance, keeping her steps light and quick. From the corner of her eye, she saw Bedlam gliding within the shadows as he kept pace with her. She felt better about going inside knowing he would be close by. It boosted her confidence so that, as she slipped through the barrier, she offered her friend a small smile in passing before plunging into the one place that had given her nightmares since the arrival of the Reapers.

Meg's lips twitched in response and she stepped out of the way as Terri entered the compound. She opened her mouth to whisper her thanks but Meg shook her head, pressing a finger to her lips as she pointed to the far corner of the camp before stepping back into the shadows, leaving Terri alone in the weak light of the encampment. Terri shivered in dread, warmed only by the press of Bedlam's hot flank to her side. Swallowing back her nerves, she too stepped into the shadows so that she might linger for a moment to survey the camp stretched out in front of her.

From where she stood, she could see tents littering the area between rusted-out cars and trucks that, by some miracle, the Reapers had managed to get running again. To the side of the trucks, a few motorcycles leaned against the remaining wall of a building that had fallen. She marveled at the collected vehicles. She hadn't realized that they had so many. Usually, when they chased after her, they never used more than two. She wondered what they were going to do when they ran out of gas. She considered trying to puncture a few fuel tanks with her knife but, despite how satisfying that would be, Terri didn't want to risk it before she found the alien.

It was a shame, though. They would find it much harder to catch their prey without vehicles.

Terri crept from her hiding spot to follow the line of cars, nearing the light of the bonfires that she could see just beyond them. Being so close to the trucks, her fingers itched to take one and strike out across the desert with it. But she would either be caught by the Reapers or die a terrible death among the sands. She didn't have the supplies, or even one of the flimsy tents dotting the encampment, to help her in her escape if she attempted it now.

A small voice in the back of her mind whispered enticingly that she could always steal one of the tents and make her getaway. She didn't need to go any farther into the camp. She wouldn't need the alien.

She squashed the voice brutally. The idea was suicidal. Someone would notice her dismantling a tent. Even studying the tents as she passed by them, most of them were occupied. No doubt the Reapers lived in the tents as there weren't many permanent structures in the compound. The few that she did see, Terri gave a wide berth, hiding among the tents as she eyed them in passing. They didn't appear to be much better than ramshackle sheds. From one of the nearby sheds, she heard women screaming and the drunken laughter of the few men who hadn't yet slipped into oblivion.

No. She wasn't about to linger; she would be caught for sure if she attempted to steal supplies. If she weren't discovered by one of the occupants of the tent, then it would certainly be by one of the men lingering eagerly around the sheds. That was something she did *not* want to happen. Best to stick with her original plan.

She passed one tent and then another, her nerves on edge. As she neared a larger tent to the fore of the cluster, she could hear loud grunts from within. She paused at the entrance and peeked inside to make sure none would look her way as she scrambled by. Her eyes widened at the view of the three occupants in profile to her. A man held a woman with frizzy blond hair beneath him, his hand over her mouth as he drove into her while his tent buddy hammered into him from behind. She stared for a moment, her curiosity overriding her common sense. She couldn't help it. It wasn't like there was a bevy of opportunities for healthy sexual experiences. At twenty-nine, she had plenty of experience manually satisfying herself. Liaisons with men had been potentially dangerous even before the Reapers arrived. She had never wanted to risk it, but she watched these three clutching at each other, expressions of affection and pleasure drifting over the faces, and envied them.

She caught herself instinctively leaning closer when Bedlam brushed his nose against her hip. This wasn't what she was here for and she didn't need the delay a distraction would cause. She closed her eyes, swallowed, and opened them to study how she would get by the tent without being seen. She couldn't unsee the fact that all three were moaning, their eyes closed with pleasure, but what she noticed now was that not one of them was facing her direction. With a whispered thanks to any higher power watching, she darted past the tent and made her way into the heart of the compound.

At the center of the camp were several large fires around which men were lying about, passed out in a drunken stupor. The central fire had a carcass hanging above the flames. The stench of burnt, fatty meat made her want to vomit. There was no wild or feral game sufficiently large enough to feed large numbers of people. The cattle had been exhausted long before people took to eating cats and dogs. Terri didn't need to guess to know what they had consumed. The remains, from what she could see, appeared to be a small human no bigger than an adolescent or petite woman. She couldn't tell if it had been male or female at one time, but it no longer mattered. She only hoped that the victim had died painlessly before being gutted and spitted.

Bedlam nosed at a broken bottle before raising his long, pointed muzzle and sniffing the air. His long ears tipped toward the fire. He whined and made a move toward the carcass but halted at her sharp, whispered command. "Bedlam, no! Come!"

Although the kid was beyond knowing that an alien dog would have been chewing on their carcass, she couldn't stomach the idea of her companion filling his belly with human flesh. Not that the dozens of Reapers lying about the fire wasn't enough of a reason to stay far away from it. Bedlam sighed and continued to pace, sniffing the air.

She narrowed her eyes as she scanned the northeastern corner of the central camp, looking for any sign of where they might keep a huge, scary-as-fuck alien. Her eyes eventually fell on a tall metal pole a few yards away near several torches. Hooked to it was a huge mass of chains facing the fire. The way the shadows fell, she couldn't get a good look at it, but the entire area around there was littered with broken bottles. She wasn't entirely certain if that was what she was looking for until Bedlam slipped through the shadows, heading directly for it.

Sand shifted under her feet as she headed toward the dark mass. She had one bad moment when a Reaper suddenly bolted upright beside where she stepped, his glazed eyes staring right at her before he slumped over again. Muttering under her breath, Terri edged closer to her destination.

Jackpot! She could barely make out the outline of the massive alien in the dark but she recognized the vague features. With a silent whoop, Terri crept around the unconscious body, studying the chains holding it down. She pinched her lips together. The padlocks were going to take some work. She had cutters back at her current bolt-hole but hadn't wanted to risk being burdened with it while trying to sneak about the Reaper camp.

Studying the chains, she followed them back to where they were clipped onto the pole. Good fortune smiled on her. It seemed that the paranoid motherfuckers had wrapped the alien in chains before attaching it to the pole, using only simple metal clips to secure it. Leaning her body against the alien's to provide some slack, she unclipped it.

The chained body fell forward against her and her knees shook with strain under the sudden weight. Heating the air with every whispered curse she could think of, Terri finally laid it flat on the ground. Pushing back upright, she scrutinized it as Bedlam circled nervously. One thing was certain: there was no way she was going to carry the unconscious alien out of the camp. She would have to drag it out.

With another muttered oath, Terri picked up the end of one heavy chain and yanked. Her arms protested as the body inched across gravel and sand. She only got a few feet before her lungs and arms began to burn painfully. She felt the sting of tears and blinked them back.

This wasn't working. Dropping the chain, she leaned over and gasped for air. Chains aside, how was it so fucking heavy? Dragging it out of the compound seemed almost impossible. Massaging her hands, Terri picked up the chain again. She barely started to tug when Bedlam appeared beside her and took another chain in its mouth. With a low growl, he pulled with far more power than she had on her own, dragging the body forward.

"Good boy," she whispered. Gently, she steered him away from the central fires, back into the deep shadows of the camp as they headed for the gates.

It was slow going, not only by design but also by need. No matter how much she wanted to rush out of the camp, she forced herself to keep a slow, steady pace, watching for any sign of Reapers. At one point, she stopped and gathered up the strange tentacles that were dragging on the ground. About as thick as ropes, they were warm, supple, and dry, textured from the tiny scales all over them like those on Bedlam's head. These, however, had tiny bulges running down the lower lengths like the end of a rattlesnake's tail. She recalled the way they had seemed to rattle with a strange, cacophonic hiss. The memory alone was enough to make her almost yank her hand away. Resolutely, she kept them gathered in her hand as they pulled the alien's unconscious body along.

By the time they neared the perimeter, the camp had settled into what she suspected was a near comatose state. Even the sounds of sex had died down to the occasional whimper until that, too, faded into exhaustion. Even with Bedlam's help, Terri's arms burned like hellfire by the time they made it back to the perimeter. She glanced at a pair of fresh skulls, still oozing with gore, before escaping the barrier.

She wouldn't miss Phoenix when she got her ride out. If the alien cooperated, that was.

By the time she arrived at her hiding place, she felt she had more than earned safe passage. It took hours of dragging to get the enormous alien all the way back to her hiding place. Although Bedlam did most of the work, she was exhausted, sore, and covered in sweat in the chill desert air. The alien had been dead weight the entire time. Not once did it even so much as twitch.

Abandoning it in the center of the room, Terri built a small fire in what remained of the hearth and threw herself on a dusty sofa. She stared at it bleakly before rousing herself enough to drag her tool bag close.

Rummaging around in the canvas, it didn't take her long to find her bolt cutters. The fact that the alien hadn't woken at all at any point during their travel didn't give her much hope for reviving it. Still, she had to try, and the first step was getting the chains off so the alien no longer looked trussed up like a Christmas turkey. Not that she had ever had one... but the pictures in the old books and ads had looked appetizing enough.

Eyeing the locks, she counted them and shook her head. Five locks, each securing a thick chain in place—a bit overkill if anyone asked her. They *really* wanted to make sure it didn't go anywhere. She cocked her head and stared down at the alien. "I wonder what exactly they thought you were going to do that couldn't be stopped with one or two chains?"

Naturally, it didn't respond. She shrugged. Oh, well. She might as well get to work.

Bedlam whined and stuck his nose in the way as he nudged at the alien. She gently pushed him back and wiped her sweaty palms on her pant legs before gripping the cutters firmly in both hands. The first lock was the worst. It was the shiniest one and resisted her attempts to cut through it. Groaning with exertion, she put all her body weight into it until the metal separated with a horribly loud *chink*. Wiping the sweat from her eyes, she scooted to the next lock, methodically moving from one lock to the next until all the locks lay scattered around the body.

The chains were another matter. They were twisted and kinked, forcing her to drag them off the alien one at a time, her feet digging into the matted carpet for leverage, cursing the Reapers for the headache they had made for her. By the time the last chain fell free, she wanted to sing her thanks to the gods above. It landed on the floor with a dull *thunk* as she let it go to rub the feeling back into her hands.

Fingers still trembling, she dug through her bag and pulled out a small bottle of oil and a tiny clay lamp. A twisted bit of an old shirt lay inside of it to serve as a wick. Although she used the lamp sparingly to conserve oil, she considered this an appropriate occasion while she attempted to assess the condition of the alien lying prone before her. She filled the lamp with a small portion of oil and struck a match. The wick soon caught fire and burned brightly, illuminating the bulk in front of her.

Leaning forward, she brushed back the mass of tentacles. The face revealed was broad and struck her as rather masculine with its square features. A cluster of small horns ran around its brow, leading up to another row of small horns that formed a crest. From the center of that, a ridge ran down, bisecting its forehead, and sloped into a broad, almost flat nose hooked with three small horns. To her surprise, the alien had a wide, human-like mouth, although not far from the corners of its lips, there were tiny hooks from serrated mandibles on its square jaw.

She leaned closer to get a better look at the mandibles when glowing blue eyes popped open and the silvery circuitry along its skin pulsed with light. Terri gasped and probably would have screamed except that its wide hand had shot up with dizzying speed and latched around her throat. The alien lifted her into the air as it got to its feet, its fingers lightly squeezing in warning as it rattled at her.

Her fingers scrambled for purchase on its strong hands as she stared down into the hellish hot blue fire of its eyes. Her eyes watered as she struggled to gasp for breath.

"Please," she wheezed.

A low growl erupted to her left and her eyes shifted downward. She couldn't crane her head to get a proper look, but she was able to make out the top of Bedlam's head as he bristled, his thin whips churning around him. The alien restraining her cocked its head to the side as it regarded its animal and uttered a confused rumble before barking out a sharp command and pointing to its feet. Bedlam whined uncertainly and glanced at her.

Blue eyes narrowed, the barely visible slit pupils focusing on her. It rumbled as it cocked its head again, this time at her. Its eyes drifted down her form and then back up again. It made a sound almost like a disgusted sigh and released her, dropping her unceremoniously to the floor. Terri wheezed as the impact took her breath away, and she spent several minutes gasping for air before she slowly sat up. Rubbing at her neck, she studied the alien quietly. It didn't kill her, so that was a step in the right direction. Instead, it sat on the broken edge of a wall, busy with self-inspection. It swung its head around as if looking for something, its mouth pulling down into a frown.

"My blaster—where is it?" it growled in a raspy voice.

Terri's mouth dropped open. It spoke English? How...? "Uh, I don't know," she said. "I didn't see anything near you when I took you out of the Reaper camp."

"Reaper," it muttered and grunted with a sound that was close to mirthful. Its eyes focused on her again. "Are you a Reaper too, little female?"

The way it dragged the last word made her shiver. "No," she whispered. "I would never be one of them."

Its expression became calculating. In her experience, that expression never boded well for her. She hastened to introduce herself. "My name is Terri."

It shifted and leaned forward. "Why?"

"I'm sorry. I don't understand."

"Why did you, a female," its lip seemed to curl at the mention of her sex, "go into territory not your own to retrieve me from the males?"

Terri saw no reason to hide the truth. "Because there's no escaping the Reapers in this city, and it's a very long way to another settlement. I want out of here."

A light of understanding dawned in the alien's eyes, and it made a chuffing sound that she suspected was laughter. It leaned closer, showing a hint of fangs as it spoke. "You desire protection."

She did not deny it. "I do. Bedlam is good protection, but even he can't save me from the Reapers if I can't get out of the city fast enough."

"Bedlam?"

She gestured to the animal, and again the alien chuffed.

"Good name," he snorted. "Bedlam, anarchy, chaos, mayhem. All translations provided in my systems would be suitable for a dorashnal. He, however, is Krono."

Krono scampered to the alien's side eagerly at the mention of his name.

Terri scooted closer, her curiosity getting the better of her. "How is it that you speak my language?"

The alien flicked a finger toward a place just in front of his ear. "Translator implant. My vessel downloaded your language files from your satellites. It proved useful when the males attempted their torture. My nanos have been learning, even when my body was forced to sleep. Learning about the Reapers and building up my resistance to their methods of caging me." Again, it chuffed with its eerie laughter. The alien didn't seem to think much of the Reapers' attempts to torture it. Its tone conveyed no little amount of mockery if she was interpreting it correctly. Had it just been waiting for an opportune moment to attack?

"You didn't need my help then," she observed.

"I did not," it agreed, tilting its head toward her.

An ember of hope lit inside of her. It might work to her benefit if she kept it curious and interested in her. It had little use for her otherwise. She licked her lips nervously. "Will you help me?"

It jerked its head away and growled. Her nerves tingled as if stuck with pins, but she resisted the urge to scramble away in fear. It wasn't acting aggressively toward her. Her only enemy at the moment was her natural fight-or-flight instinct when faced with an obviously superior predator. The tentacle whips around its head swelled. "I am here to salvage, nothing more. This planet was not supposed to be inhabited by a living civilization."

Terri snorted. "Well, in all fairness, it's not really a civilization any longer. All that's left on Earth are scattered settlements and a few roaming caravans. A few tribal groups have managed to survive from what I've been told. I don't know. I've never been outside Phoenix. I'm not sure if it is any better on other parts of the planet, but I suspect not. From what my grandparents told me, our series of World Wars pretty much wiped us out, even those who tried to remain uninvolved."

The alien muttered to itself in another language before leveling her with an irritated stare. "My sensors failed to detect a sentient presence, but your species is living in primitive means below sustainability. Those who do not adapt will cease to exist."

She winced, but it was nothing that she hadn't considered herself. Human civilization had fallen and was long gone. Even the planet was barely limping along, judging by the freak storms that often raged. Like a host determined to get rid of a parasite, their planet was correcting itself, renewing, and killing off most of the humans. More died every year.

She considered her options. She had nothing to give, and obviously she would only amuse the alien for short stretches of time before it would likely become disinterested in her presence.

She needed to offer something useful.

"You said you're here to salvage. What if I help you?"

That got its attention. The alien whipped its head around, its brow dipped in contemplation.

She hurried to make her pitch. She would do anything to get out of Phoenix, even pick through trash for parts. "I mean, obviously you can handle the Reapers, but I'm sure you want to get done quickly. With twice as many hands working, you can get out of here faster with your load. And when you leave, you can just drop me off someplace on your way out."

It tapped one of its thick fingers on its knee in a human-like gesture as it considered her offer. Bedla—no, Krono, looked up from where it lay at his master's feet. She barely dared to breathe as the alien considered her and her offer.

Finally, it let out a low growl and sat back. "Very well. Agreed."

Terri sat down and settled against her pack with a smile. That was all she needed. Her imagination immediately conjured up images of the coast. Miles of sparkling beach with blue waves breaking across it. If humanity was a dying species where only the most resilient were destined to survive, she wouldn't mind spending her last days beside the ocean. She would greet her ending by the fierce appetite of Mother Nature rather than by the hands of marauders and the mad.

"What is your name?" she finally asked. She couldn't keep calling it alien.

"I am Veral'monushava'skahalur of Argurumal." She stared and moved her lips as she turned the name around in her mind. She didn't think she even caught half of it. It chuffed again. "Veral. You may call me Veral, little human, Terri of Earth."

"Well, Veral, we'd better move into one of the other rooms with four walls where we can get some sleep. I don't know about you, but dealing with spiders and scorpions is bad enough. Dirt blowing into my eyes and mouth while I sleep is something I try to avoid. I'd rather wake up without that… assuming you aren't going to murder me in my sleep," she added worriedly.

Veral chuffed again as it stood and followed her farther back into the dwelling.

"Do not worry, human. You will not die this night."

"Comforting," she muttered.

They settled into what was clearly once a nursery. She was surprised that it didn't pick another room but instead seemed content to keep her within eyesight. Or maybe her alien was just that suspicious.

Terri wanted to laugh as she checked the area for nasty critters before finally settling down. Unable to keep her eyes open any longer, she pulled a thin blanket out of her bag. Wrapping it around herself, she ignored the pang of guilt that she had nothing for her alien companion and settled down to sleep.

6

*T*erri woke to the smoky scent of meat and discovered that Veral had left while she was sleeping and returned not only with meat that the alien was patiently roasting over the fire, but with two metal carts filled with various metal parts. The alien hunched over them, its brow furrowed as it dug through them, likely checking to make sure that everything that it collected was still there and accounted for. Seemingly satisfied, it nodded and rose to its full height to walk the short distance to the fire.

Terri stared longingly at the large, fat lizards skewered over the fire. Her stomach grumbled. She hadn't had fresh meat for a very long time. She'd tried catching lizards before but they were too quick for her. Her eyes trailed over to where Krono lay in a corner with his own, tearing it apart hungrily. She swallowed back her saliva. She wasn't going to assume that Veral intended to share with her. She didn't catch them, after all.

Ignoring the smell of cooking meat, she dug into her pack and pulled out a tin of SPAM. She pulled the tab and grimaced at the slimy contents. Eating the sludgy meat was less appealing than ever. She poked at it and started when Veral chuffed.

"Do not eat that vizi," the alien growled as it thrust a skewer at her. "That is not food. This is food. Eat."

Setting the can down, she gratefully accepted the skewer, her mouth watering from the aroma.

"What's vizi?" she asked as she blew on the hot meat to cool it.

Veral huffed and regarded her with amusement. "Vizi is a way of saying the foulest of the foul. By the smell alone, I can tell that whatever that is, it is barely edible."

Terri pinched off some of the seared, flaky skin and stuffed her mouth full of the tender meat. It burned her tongue, but the flavor was so welcoming that she moaned with pleasure. Veral glanced up at her at the sound, the whips around his head puffing out as he watched her. She gave him a sheepish look as she stuffed more into her mouth.

"Sorry," she mumbled around the meat. "It's been so long since I had real meat. This is delicious."

The alien continued to stare, frozen in place, before making a low trilling sound and turning its attention back to its own food. As she ate, she watched in fascination out of the corner of her eye, trying not to stare as Veral's mandibles widened as its mouth opened to receive food. The sharp, serrated mandibles seemed to cut through the meat even as they guided it into the alien's mouth, where the chunks were chewed a time or two before he swallowed. It was both a fascinating and unsettling sight.

Clearing her throat, Terri looked away and nodded to the carts in the middle of what was left of the living room. "So, what's all that?"

Veral grunted and gestured to the nearest cart. "Quality scrap metal."

Obviously a being of few words. Terri continued to chew as she leaned forward to glance into the cart nearest her. One section was filled with random bits of metal, while another held works of art. She raised an eyebrow as she looked at Veral's findings.

"You actually get paid for this junk?"

Veral swallowed the last bites of its meal and jerked its head roughly in the affirmative. It was less a human nod and more a rapid circular motion of its head that culminated in a downward tip of its chin. The motion sent the whips on the back of its head moving.

"The metals are accumulated and melted down. The relics are bought by collectors. Many credits to be made from simple salvage."

"Wow, incredible! It's almost hard to believe." She grinned at Veral and the alien stilled, its mandibles widening as it bared its teeth at her with a threatening rattle. Her smile wilted and alarm surged through her. But she refused to be cowed. Instead, she glared up at it. The alien's whips writhed in a clear show of dominance. Her skin shivered in reaction, but she didn't back down.

Finally, Veral chuffed and leaned back, giving her another peculiar nod.

"You are brave, but do not threaten one who is stronger unless you are prepared to fight," Veral admonished her with another loud chuffing sound.

Terri's mouth dropped open. "I wasn't challenging you. I was *smiling*!"

The alien narrowed its eyes on her. "That is not a smile. This is a smile." It gestured to its mouth as its lips twisted upward as the corners, seeming to align with the tips of its mandibles, making the smile all the more unsettling and alien.

"Humans smile that way too, kind of, but we also smile more fully like this." She demonstrated by grinning at him again, although this time it felt considerably more strained.

"Humans are a strange species. Very well… if you insist." She laughed at his grudging acceptance, and the alien's bright eyes fastened at her before something behind them seemed to soften with humor.

It was a start.

With a chirp to Krono, Veral turned to head out to the street, leaving Terri to scramble to her feet and follow after them.

Outside, the alien stretched, seemingly soaking in the sun before it reached for its belt and unclipped three large, dull gray discs. Veral showed them to her before putting one on the ground.

With a touch to a band around its wrist, the disc unfolded into the familiar shape of one of his carts.

"Once these three are filled, we will return the units to the cargo hold on my ship and retrieve more."

Terri scratched her nose where her latest sunburn was peeling. "How much are you planning on salvaging? To be honest, there are a great many cities on this planet. You could spend a lifetime here salvaging for scraps and still not get everything."

"My storage only has room for twenty units of cargo. Once I have filled my ship to maximum capacity, I will alert a team to the coordinates. They will continue to salvage while paying out a percentage to my accounts while I search for other salvage opportunities."

Terri's eyebrows flew up. "Wow, that must be lucrative."

"It is satisfying," Veral said.

They went from residence to residence, looking for bits of metal, circuitry, art, and jewelry. More often than not, she found herself forced to pry open old electronics and pull out the tiny metal bits. These she deposited in the cart. There were some metals that Veral wasn't interested in. Copper seemed to interest the alien the most whereas steel wasn't bothered with. She discovered that after Veral threw out the set of knives she'd put in the bins. The result was that, even after hours of working, there was barely more than a few inches of shiny metal at the bottom of the first bin. Her back ached and her mood was souring. Reminding herself that she had a free ride to the coast coming her way, she kept silent and continued to work at a driven pace.

For the most part, they worked side-by-side wordlessly. The alien rarely spoke except to issue commands to Krono when he began to wander. It took them a full day to half-fill one of the carts. Terri found that depressing. It was almost tempting to recant on her offer and make tracks while she could, but then she reminded herself that there was a huge expanse of merciless desert between her and the coast. Even if it took a week to gather salvage, it was preferable to attempting that trek. So she continued to work without complaint, and in the evening they went back to their shelter, where Veral left her in order to hunt for their evening meal. Eating regularly almost compensated for her sore muscles.

They soon fell into a routine, spending the days filtering through the remains of hollowed-out homes, looking for anything that the Reapers hadn't already taken. The alien's constant, silent presence felt more comforting even though she didn't know anything more about it than she had when they met. She'd tried to engage Veral in conversation, but her companion only spoke to issue orders, which became more and more annoying as the days passed. Despite that, she grew accustomed to its inhuman features, and that lessened her fear of Veral, making her increasingly bold.

She blamed that as the reason she finally snapped impatiently when the alien had—once again, for the hundredth time—grunted and gestured to a corner of a room that they were picking through.

"Pointing at something and grunting doesn't tell me what you want very well. You're going to have at least try to talk to me," she retorted in exasperation as she threw down her bag. She immediately snapped her mouth shut, almost biting her tongue when Veral's eyes narrowed at her, a menacing sound dragging up from the back of his throat. A cold sweat popped over her skin, but she didn't move as it paced closer to her in an attempt to intimidate her.

She had no doubt that dominance displays were in equal part a way to control her and a form of entertainment given how frequent they had become. Still, this time Terri knew she'd finally pushed the alien too far and that it was about to kill her and leave her carcass for the buzzards. Her muscles tightened and twitched anxiously. Yet, to her surprise, Veral snapped the whips draping from its head with a loud hiss before gesturing again.

"Search over there, female, through the remaining debris for anything of value. Let us be on our way before night comes." The alien turned away from her and stalked over to another area, tossing furniture out of his way, and he dug back through the more difficult section of the room where a wall had caved in.

Her lips quirked and a wave of endorphins flooded her system after escaping that confrontation unscathed. "See? That didn't hurt you any, did it?" Her eyes widened in horror as she pressed her lips together and cursed her mouth which apparently had a death wish.

The alien snapped around, its whips flaring around its head as it glared at her. She smiled sheepishly and scampered to her duty before the alien second-guessed its decision not to kill her for her impertinence.

Clamping her lips shut, lest she provoke its ire again, she worked tirelessly throughout the day. She was rummaging through a big bin when he shifted a large section of a crumbling wall with a loud snarl. She stopped, squinting through the dust at Veral as the alien stepped into what had obviously been some sort of storage space. The growl turned into an interested trill as Veral pulled something out and set it on the floor.

Curious, Terri crept forward, waving one hand through the air to disperse the dust motes and plaster fragments away from her face. What did Veral have there? She walked over and leaned forward to see around the alien's massive body. She hadn't even been aware that she brushed against her companion until it jerked and whirled on her, its whips snapping around it so aggressively that one caught her across the cheek before she managed to scramble away to a safe distance.

Bringing one hand up to her bleeding face, she stared at the alien in shock.

Veral snarled and shook its head aggressively but it crept closer, its eyes inspecting her face. "You are damaged," it observed gruffly.

"I was only trying to see what you found and you sliced the hell out of me!"

A low hiss came from its throat. "My apologies. I reacted instinctively. Never touch an Argurma uninvited. Make certain you remember this. Humans are very fragile, it appears," it murmured, its eyes softening slightly. "Now hold still. I will heal you this time."

"Heal me? How?" she asked.

"With my saliva."

Veral's long, dark tongues emerged then from its mouth, the

pair twining and flexing, the tapered tips oddly flexible. She wrinkled her nose as it leaned forward. The alien's breath didn't smell bad like she expected it would. Instead, it had a curious spicy scent. Its two tongues lashed forward, slipping over her skin, depositing a trail of something sticky where they touched her wound. She lifted a hand to explore the cut, but Veral grabbed her by the wrist and held her still while the substance dried. Only then did the alien release her. Glaring at him, she ran her fingers over a hard, raised trail.

"The cut is sealed. In two days, my hormonal saliva will crack and fall away, leaving only healed skin in its place," Veral grunted before turning away from her once more to empty the contents of what she now saw were several lockboxes cracked open.

Terri cleared her throat awkwardly and wandered back to where she'd been working once more. She hated to admit that she spent the rest of the day tiptoeing around the big alien, but Veral really did prefer maintaining its own personal space and she had no problem giving that. She probably went overboard, venturing nowhere near touching distance, but that was her prerogative, even if on several occasions she felt his eyes watching her curiously. Despite the fact that those whips didn't hurt more than a papercut, she was determined to not risk a repeat performance.

When they returned to their shelter that night, they huddled once again in a shared room. Veral never attempted to lay closer than a foot or two away from her. She almost wished the alien would. The temperature dropped at night in the desert, and the body heat would have been welcomed. She suspected that Veral didn't suffer from it the way she did, the same way that the alien never seemed to be uncomfortable even in the midday sun that sent Terri looking for shelter to wait out the worse hours.

It was late into the fifth day salvaging that she heard the familiar roar of a Reaper engine, and Terri froze. It was some distance away, probably chasing after other "prey," but she couldn't ignore the gut instinct to run and hide. If it weren't for the fact that she didn't want to seem like a complete waste of space to the alien standing stoically nearby, she would have. If Veral was unconcerned, she had little reason to worry. They had a bargain, and she didn't think the alien would just abandon her to be captured. She shrugged it off and continued searching through the rubble of an old cinema.

The alien didn't seem to be fooled by her pretense of nonchalance. Veral turned and looked at her, bony brow raising with interest. "You are afraid of them."

"Well, yes, of course I am. I'd be suicidal to not be at least a little afraid of them. They would capture me if they had the opportunity."

"They hunted you that day."

She had no need to ask what day Veral was speaking of. "They tried to," she said.

"You survived and, even though you were afraid, you still entered their abode and freed me."

"Yes."

Veral considered her in silence for a few minutes, its blue eyes never shifting away from her. Suddenly, its lips tilted up in a closed-lipped smile and it nodded.

"You are fierce, Terri... for a human," Veral amended with a loud chuff of laughter.

Terri smiled in return, flattered despite the indirect insult to her species. She stretched her back, her loose shirt pulling taut as she attempted to ease her muscles. Veral's blue eyes shifted to her before again focusing on its work. She thought she'd seen something flicker in that gaze, but shrugged it off—she was likely mistaken. They continued to work in companionable silence for the rest of the evening.

It was very late at night when they heard another engine rev nearby, this time passing so close to the house they were sleeping in that it woke Terri up. Her heart pounded wildly in her chest and fear seeped out of every pore as she heard the laughter of Reapers. She nearly jumped out of her skin when she felt a warm, dry hand on her shoulder. She skittered to the side and glanced behind her, meeting Veral's luminous eyes.

The alien's pointed ears shifted forward in their limited range of motion. Although Veral's head turned slightly as a rat scurried by in the dark, the alien's focus was entirely on the noises outside their hiding place. A loud crash near the door made Terri jump, but Veral's arm banded around her, steadying her. A single hand stroked her hair soothingly as it whispered to her in a low voice.

"Males seek females. Breeding is a prerogative among most species in the universe. The impulse to hunt out one's mate doesn't cease to exist because one's civilization falls. Perhaps the need becomes even greater then. I do not know. It is a natural desire, but they seek to terrorize females. I do not approve of this. The Argurma are not gentle mates, but even we are not so cruel. Do not worry. I will protect you."

She shivered and leaned against the alien, allowing its warmth to flow into her body. She needed the distraction, so she asked the first question that came to mind.

"Have you ever had a mate?"

Silence descended between them, and Terri worried that she'd asked a taboo question. At length, she heard a raspy sigh. "I came close once, but my intended decided in the end to pair with another. Mating is competitive. No male is guaranteed that a female will choose them, and every male desires the best female. If you were Argurma, you would have been courted by hundreds of males. Your nature is strong like ours. Many would have desired to impress you, even if you have a kindness in you that my people would consider a debilitating weakness. Yet, I find even that I like."

Terri grinned in the darkness, forgetting that Veral could see her. As always, her alien stiffened as she bared her teeth but was reacting less every time she smiled. She tensed as a small, nagging thought filtered through her brain.

Veral had informed her in not so many words that he was male, and that as a male, he was showing admiration for her by comparing her to the females of his world. She no longer felt threatened in his company beyond the dissipating unease she usually felt. Truth be told, she felt far safer with him than with any human male. She pulled back as she eyed the alien beside her.

"You're male?" she whispered.

Veral bristled in offense, his arms tightening protectively around her. "Yes."

She couldn't think of anything to say to that. It didn't bother her, so it seemed pointless to make a big deal out of it. Instead, she wanted to enjoy the offered comfort. She leaned forward and rested her head against his chest. His body tensed beneath her and his skin seemed to shudder where her breath brushed it. He didn't object and, if she wasn't mistaken, it felt like he settled more comfortably against her. The strange rhythm of his heart filled her ear, providing a soothing sound that drowned out whatever noise the Reapers were making on the streets.

She felt… safe.

"Oh, okay," she mumbled against his chest. She could feel the tension easing out of him even as her own body relaxed. Terri yawned, and to her surprise he didn't pull away to his customary place. This time, he continued to hold her long after the sounds of Reapers had faded and sleep had claimed her.

7

*V*eral followed the small human down the road. Like every other street, it was cracked in many places. Appropriate for a city of crumbling buildings. The species was dying as assuredly as the city was returning to the sands. Even the humans he had seen appeared to be barely clinging to life. Although the Reapers had spoken of pregnant females, he couldn't imagine offspring thriving in such desolation.

Not that he had seen any since his arrival. All he'd seen were fragments of playthings. The sight had brought a hazy feeling to him that he couldn't quite define. Like fragments of his past drifting on his conscious mind seeking to reclaim him.

Veral barely recalled any details from his youth before his first cybernetic implants. It was intentionally engineered in such a way that a cybernetic citizen would feel loyalty first and always to their state. They weren't meant to remember their families or their past. Veral was fortunate enough that sometimes a memory would rise up and flood his processors with the colors, flavors, and emotions of his youth, but it was always fleeting, and faded before he could even attempt to grasp it.

Yet he'd been aware that it set him apart distinctly, and had led to his eventual rebellion from his homeworld when he realized just how much was taken from him. It was something all Argurma accepted… except him. But he was accustomed to being different and having to hide it among his brethren. Being different was not approved of. He would be seen as malfunctioning, and quarantined by the doctors for testing to root out the source of his malfunction. He kept away from his own to keep his secret and hold onto the memories as best he could when they came.

When he'd held Terri to reduce her stress, one such memory floated to the surface. It seemed to last longer when he touched her and so he'd been loath to release her even after the danger passed. It was a hazy memory of his mother. She'd been holding him in her arms, whispering to him comfortingly as a storm had raged. He could almost recall the tang of fear as lightning flashed through the room, and the warm, solid presence of his mother. So he'd clung to Terri, trying desperately to retain the memory.

Unfortunately, though it had lingered longer than others, it too eventually passed. He didn't know why he continued to hold the female after that. Perhaps he'd hoped another memory would come.

The memory, however, made the absence of offspring even more noticeable. Offspring meant life, hope, and the continuation of a species. Not all chose to breed, but the creation of offspring was necessary to maintain a healthy population. So far, he'd seen and heard many adult humans. The females he saw less of, but heard and scented them in the camp once he'd been able to identify them. He knew that there were pregnant females, but not one infant or juvenile below the age of adolescence. The absence of young didn't strike him as particularly consequential until now.

"Why are there no human offspring?"

Terri startled and glanced at him. She lifted one shoulder and her lips twisted as if to smile, but she scented of sadness, belying her expression. He frowned at her, confused as to why she didn't give the proper expressions for her emotions. She looked away into the distance for a short time before answering.

"It's been quite a few years since anyone has birthed living babies," she said at last. "Women get pregnant often enough, especially, I imagine, within the Reaper camp, but no one to my knowledge has been able to carry to term. Hard to say why that is. Perhaps it's what we're eating, or our living conditions." She shook her head and climbed over a fallen wall. He watched her, noting that her face was reddening from the sun at an alarming rate once again before the damaged skin had time to completely slough off. There were creams that some of the other salvagers applied before working in similar environments, but he didn't carry any on his ship since he did not require them.

"What about you?" she asked, making him jerk so slightly that he doubted she noticed.

"I do not understand your question," he grumbled, disliking being caught off guard.

She laughed softly. "I mean, do you have any childr—offspring?"

"It is forbidden," he stated with finality. "I am unmated and unlicensed from the planetary register for donating genetic material."

Her delicate hairs on her brow arched up at him as her lips twisted with obvious amusement. "Donating genetic material? You don't give it up directly?"

He scowled at the female at his side. "Give what up? Your words are not precise enough for me to know what you are asking."

"Uh, you know, make offspring the way nature intended. Male meets female, and they mate and create little offspring naturally."

He stared at her, aghast. Oh, he knew that at how other species did it, but to suggest that Argurma behave in such a way was absurd. "We are an advanced and enlightened species, superior to most organic species in every way. Our society determined long ago that to manufacture the strongest offspring, mated pairs with a license to do so submit their genetic material."

"That doesn't sound fun," she said. He wasn't sure if she

intended to mock the ways of his people, or if she seriously believed that fun had anything to do with it.

"Reproduction is a serious matter," he returned shortly. "It is not intended for enjoyment or amusement if one is vested in procreation. Choosing the best genetic samples from the mated pair provides strong, healthy offspring."

He didn't miss her incredulous look. "I guess, although that sounds too cold and clinical. As far as I am concerned, children are a blessing regardless of how they come. If I had any, I wouldn't need them to be the best to love them."

He snorted suspiciously. "And what if they were flawed in a way that made them different?"

She lifted a shoulder again in what he was beginning to suspect was something between a dismissal and uncertainty, depending on the question. "Then they would be unique."

Veral cocked his head at her, caught off-guard by her apparent sincerity.

Females of his species would never admit to such feelings even if they had them. A female was to desire strong healthy offspring who would honorably continue her lineage.

He didn't want to admit to Terri that his mating had failed because the female he was courting learned that his mother had been isolated as malfunctioning and eventually terminated when her emotional compulsions could not be corrected.

Terri kicked a dead lump of plant life out of her way. "Okay then, so offspring are grown in labs for this faulty idea of perfection. Then what? I suppose you have a rigid education and all that. Shit that no one here cares about because we're too busy surviving." She paused and scrubbed her hands on her pants. "I can read," she said. "Not a lot, since my mother died when I was young, but she taught me a little." She gave him a sidelong glance and smiled humorlessly. "I suppose that would make me even more inferior."

His vibrissae twitched. "There is no comparison between other races, who do not seek out perfection, and the Argurma. It would not be held against you. We are held to higher standards, which includes education from infancy to produce the best warriors, technicians, and scientists. Sometimes a mated pair feels inclined to rear their offspring to such expectations, but usually Argurma young are raised in age groups for social conditioning and educational purposes. Upon reaching adulthood, it is supplemented with technology that further increases our abilities."

"Wow," she said, laughter noticeably lacing her tone. He found the sound intriguing and enjoyed hearing though he suspected that she was mocking him. "I see you didn't include anything remotely artistic or compassionate in that list. As for it not being held against me, I'm not sure if that is a backhanded compliment or a really shitty xenophobic observation. See? I know a few big words too."

Terri glared at him for a moment before huffing, her eyes trained on a building just up ahead. Veral followed her attention to the sloping roof of a collapsed building. It appeared to be buckled in the front and rear, blocking off much of the lower level. The ground level, however, was impenetrable stone. His lip curled at the inconvenience, his eyes landing on a collapsed porch and staircase that disappeared under rubble. He lifted his gaze to the level above that and noticed a broken window, leaving a gap far too small for his large frame. He circled around to the back of the building and found the conditions much the same, and all the windows on the main floor just above him were locked firmly in place.

"This house is pretty unusual in Phoenix. Someone must have paid big money to have it rebuilt here," Terri said as she paced around the building, studying it intently. "We're going to have to get in the hard way. The access to the daylight basement and main floor is completely blocked off. Looks like broken window it is!"

He frowned at the back of her head. If she got hurt, he would not be able to go in to pull her out. He opened his mouth to object and remind her of her obligation of assisting him when she suddenly spoke.

"So which group did you belong to?" she asked.

He blinked, blindsided by the question. It didn't take any substantial guesswork to know what she meant, despite the quick change of subject after their prolonged silence preceding it.

He didn't look at her as he replied curtly, "I was reared by my mother."

Terri glanced over at him. "What about your father?"

"My sire provided all the required necessities, but the female rules the domicile. All offspring are attached to her, so when a mated pair decides to rear their young, it is her responsibility and the adult offspring, in the end, will reflect on her line. My mother wished to rear me, and my father yielded to her wish, though he had no desire to take part. It is not an unusual arrangement among Argurma who choose to raise their offspring."

Turning to face him fully, Terri's lips dropped in an expression of sadness that he failed to understand. Looking away, she focused on the building, blinking her eyes rapidly. Veral expanded his mandibles, drawing in her complex scent.

The unmistakable wet tang of sadness and a layer of something else undefinable.

"Why are you sad, female?" he demanded with a flare of impatience when she remained silent, her eyes scouting along the perimeter of the building. Although it was reasonable to be attentive to the lay of the area, the scent was lingering, and it disturbed him that she did not attempt to explain it.

Terri turned her eyes on him with annoyance as her lips twisted in displeasure. "Jeez, you're pushy. If you want to know something, can't you ask nicely?"

"My query was expedient," he replied, his brow dropping into a scowl.

She shook her head at him and returned her attention to the roof, her lips tightening. "If you lift me up, I think I can wiggle in through the window and look around to see if there's anything worth tossing outside to you."

Not one to be deflected, Veral crossed his arms over his chest and glowered, his lips tightening even as his mandible opened in irritation. When he didn't reply, Terri glanced over at him and rolled her eyes.

"If you are so set on knowing, then fine, I'll tell you. That you speak of your father as if his presence was more or less inconsequential makes me miss what I had with my father before the Reapers killed him. He was all I had after my mother died. I'm sad for myself... and for you," she said quietly.

Veral drew back, his vibrissae puffing out aggressively. He felt both attacked by her soft-spoken admission and destroyed by it. He had seen since leaving Argurumal the way males of other species behaved with their offspring, even among other salvagers who took their families with them. It plucked at something within him that he'd been unable to identify, and yet with this female's simple declaration, a sense of loss surged within him from nowhere. His processor grappled with it, trying to understand this feeling. He knew anger and pain. He knew something of the bitter humor which got him through many difficult times and vengeance. Loss was the product of an unnecessary attachment.

"I do not require your pity," he stated. "I do not recall much of my sire, or even my mother in my youth. Such attachments are unnecessary. Mate bonds are the only reasonable and permissible attachment as it guarantees a consistent and stable breeding pair while providing a regular companion for psychological health. That need has not been something our designers have been able to get around, and so our males and females are required to mate when we are young adults."

She lifted a speculative eyebrow. "That is... disturbing. That's the nicest thing I can honestly think to say. It seems like a very cold existence, although at least you can have a mate. How old are you, anyway?"

"Not young," he retorted with a snap of his vibrissae.

"And is your mental health declining?" she asked, a tiny smile playing on her lips.

"No," he said. He could feel his vibrissae flattening against his skull defensively.

He did not like that this female was bringing so many emotional reactions from him. He desired nothing but his comfort and his wealth. He didn't need to be hampered with inconvenient emotions.

Her teeth immediately bared in a wide, savage smile. "So there's no reason not to tell me. Come on," she coaxed. "How old?"

He growled, willing her to back down despite the kernel of pleasure and admiration at her bold insistence. Her smile became sharper, more like a snarl, and the lines of her face set in determination. His vibrissae flicked humorously and he broke out into a loud chuffing.

"Very well, anastha. I am two hundred fifty-seven."

Her lips pursed and she whistled through them. "That's fucking ancient compared to humans. And just how old are your people when you normally mate?"

He grumbled the number under his breath. She leaned forward, a smile curving her lips as her eyes shone humorously.

"I'm sorry… What was that?"

"Eighty-nine planetary revolutions," he grunted.

The humor in her eyes died as she leaned back to regard him somberly. "That is a very long time to be alone."

Veral threw back his shoulders and puffed out his vibrissae with pride, his mandible spread in a show of power as he glared down at her. "I do not require such attachments to be operational. I have no malfunctions and am at peak performance—or was until I was recently damaged, but my nanos are repairing me, and my vengeance will be visited upon them before I leave this world."

"Uh-huh," she said, her brows winging upward. "That's some pretty intense denial. By the way, what does anastha mean?" she asked, changing the direction of conversation. Veral didn't know if he should be grateful or insulted that she felt necessary to deflect. What he did experience was embarrassment at her poor pronunciation mangling such an esteemed term.

"Anastha," he repeated slowly, emphasizing the sharp click following the "n" and "th."

Terri repeated it back to him. The clicks sounded muffled to him rather than sharp and concise, but it was at least an improvement. His lips twitched at her concentration as she devoted herself to sounding the word out under her breath.

"What does it mean?" she asked again.

"It is a term that translates to 'fierce one,'" he replied. She bared her teeth with such pleasure that for the first time he didn't feel his vibrissae tingle and twitch in response to what would normally have been an expression of challenge. Instead, the odd warmth returned again, and his lips curved in response. She thankfully didn't see it as she turned her back to him to inspect the building once more.

"I like that," she said with a distinct sound of satisfaction. "Okay, now boost this 'fierce one' up so I can take a look."

"Negative," he responded firmly.

She looked over her shoulder at him, a puzzled expression on her face as her pink lips dropped at the corners. "Excuse me?"

"We have a bargain for your assistance. I cannot follow you within to make sure you are not harmed. Letting you go in alone is disadvantageous for me when I could potentially lose your assistance."

Terri stared askance at him and then snorted out a laugh. "I see why you're encouraged to mate. You need someone to fuss over. You don't need to worry about me, though. I've been in and out of these buildings all my life. Now help me up!"

Veral was not fussing, nor did he require anyone to fuss over. Yes, it was satisfying to have someone need his presence rather than just tolerating him, but that was all.

He did not require a female. Although he barely saw his sire after his mother's termination, he was aware that the male eventually been found deceased in their dwelling before the first year was out, lunars after his failed courtship. Although it was exceedingly rare, that dependency alarmed him, and he considered himself fortunate to have not been chosen. Most healthy mates survived the passing of a mate, but he and his line had already proved to be flawed.

He would be in the minority who would be dangerously attached.

With a low snarl, he stomped forward and set his hands upon Terri's hips, ignoring the startling shock that tingled through his hands and up his arms at the contact. "Very well. If you insist on being foolish, I shall comply. I advise you to avoid harm. I will be severely displeased otherwise."

erri squawked in surprise when Veral effortlessly—and at a speed she hadn't been prepared for—lifted her to the edge of the sloping roof. On her hands and knees, with her fingers digging into the shingles, she shuffled over to the one visible window of what had once been the fourth-floor attic space of the house. The window was smaller than she'd assumed when looking at it from the ground but still large enough to squeeze through—if just barely. For a moment, she didn't want to go in. The interior was dark, and she caught traces of some kind of horrible smell coming from it.

Her throat working in a desperate attempt not to retch, Terri gripped the edge of the window and pulled herself inside, wiggling in such a fashion that she easily dropped within. She regretted her decision almost immediately when she landed on something that squelched beneath her as it folded under her weight. The musty smell of rotting wood and fabric flooded her nose.

How the hell did something wet end up in the attic? It hadn't rained in months.

"Female?" Veral's voice drifted up to her.

"You know damn well my name is Terri!" she shouted down,

the distance giving her bravado an edge that it didn't have when she was face-to-face with the intimidating alien.

He grunted in response. "Clearly you are well."

"I'd be better if it didn't stink so bad here. Fuck, it smells like something died." She gagged as the nauseating smell of death bore down on her even stronger.

"The entire city carries the stink of death," Veral said.

True enough. Setting down her pack, she felt around until she came across her lamp, and her small bundle that contained a portion of oil, flint, and steel. Setting the lamp down, she filled it and after a few attempts caught the wick with an ember, sending a soft light illuminating the tiny area around her. Picking up the lamp in one hand, she lifted it and stepped forward only to pale and stumble back. She couldn't hold it in this time; she bent over and puked until her throat burned and nothing more came up but bitter stomach acid.

"Anastha?"

She rolled her eyes upward but admitted it was better than being called "female." It was actually kind of sweet in a weird way.

"I'm all right. There's just… *fuck*… there are a lot of dead people in this attic."

She felt another wave of nausea as she looked at the bloody mess she'd made of the body she landed on. Her hand shook as she lifted the lamp closer to the decomposing body and blanched. Aside from the damage that she'd accidentally done, the body had huge bites taken out of it that made her stomach roil. Turning slowly, she lifted the lamp higher and crept to every single body, four in total, to inspect the remains. All of them had terrible bite wounds.

"Fuck," she whispered, her eyes widening as her mouth filled with saliva and her throat worked sickeningly. "These people look like they've been eaten!" she called down to Veral. Silence greeted her observation until a low, angry snarl followed her into the cramped room from below.

"Retreat. Get out of there now!" Veral snapped.

"Yeah," she mumbled, "I think that may be a good idea."

Turning back to the window, she took two steps and the wood creaked loudly under her weight. Terri froze, her legs braced wide apart and she stared wide-eyed at her exit still too far away.

"Female!" Veral shouted, his voice literally vibrating with anger as it carried to her through the dark room.

"Veral..." she whispered as a deafening crack surrounded her. A high-pitched shriek came out of her mouth as the floor gave way beneath her and sent her hurtling down below.

Rotten floorboards and dust fell all around her as her hip and rib cage slammed against the floor of the third-level hallway. Her breath rushed out of her in a wheeze. Choking on the thick dust, she gagged and drew in a long, unsteady breath to regain control of herself between hacking coughs that sent spasms through her body until they settled. Distantly, she could hear Veral shouting her name as she lay there staring up at the broken ceiling.

With a painful groan, Terri rolled over onto her belly and pulled her elbows and knees beneath her before slowly pushing herself onto her hands and knees, and then finally to her feet. Bending over, she picked up her oil lamp, the flames thankfully extinguished by her fall, and set it upright before refilling and lighting it.

Light spilled through the corridor, showing off the faded wallpaper. She recoiled from a dark patch staining the floor and wall near a room, the door of which had been left ajar. She began to back away from the door before she caught herself and swiped a hand down her face. Obviously, whatever had happened there was some time ago. It was unlikely that anything dangerous still remained in the room, if it had even been inside there at all. There was a thick coating of dust undisturbed on everything. Whatever had eaten the bodies upstairs must not have left the attic—at least as far as she could tell. As both the far ends of the hallway were collapsed, that didn't leave her with very many options for a starting place. She might as well start there.

Stepping around a dried bloodstain, Terri pushed her way through the door. The room itself, though covered with dust, was elegant as if caught in time. Although yellowed with age, white lace and linens graced with what once had to have been lush comforters adorned the room against what appeared to be a pink wallpaper that was browning in many places.

Holding her sack tightly against her shoulder, she crept through the room, her fingers skimming over surfaces. On one chair, a pile of teddy bears watched her through smudged glass eyes as she explored the space. Despite being watched by her inanimate audience, she ignored them, a wide smile breaking over her face as she came across a jewelry box set in the corner of a large wooden vanity.

Tilting up the lid, she jumped and nearly dropped it when a mechanism moved, sending a few notes of a melody chiming out of it. It sang so cheerfully in the empty quiet of the room that she could hear a trace echo of the brief melody in the house. Enchanted, she thrust the box into her bag instead of just upending it like she'd planned. Working her way through the room, she picked over the offerings, tossing anything that Veral could possibly have use for into her bag. When thoroughly scouting through the room offered nothing else of possible value, she slipped back out the door and proceeded to the next room.

A room in shades of blue ended up being a complete waste of her time. Despite its palette of restful hues, it seemed like no one had resided in that room. She settled for stripping a tiny frame painting of flowers and another of an ocean scene off the walls before departing. The other two rooms weren't much better. They both had large open bags sitting on their beds, although each bedside stand held personal electronics that she broke before removing their delicate inner pieces.

Burdened with the pleasant weight of her findings, Terri hummed a tune, almost able to forget the grisly scene upstairs. Almost. It kept intruding into her thoughts like an unwelcome visitor, reminding her there was something not quite right about the entire scenario. She descended the dark stairs, each step creaking ominously underfoot. She paused at the first one and breathed a sigh of relief as it held. Not wanting to tempt misfortune, she sped down the stairs, stepping as lightly as possible. It wasn't until she was panting at the bottom of the steps, safely on the second floor — really the main floor since the first floor had appeared to once have been a large garage and daylight basement — that the thought which had been niggling in the back of her mind came to the fore.

All the blood and decaying bodies. It wasn't right. It didn't fit with what was normal in Phoenix if it happened some time ago. It had been oddly fresh… the desert typically dried corpses out quickly. Wood rot was expected, not mushy corpses. That meant that whoever it had been must have been in and out of the house recently. There had to be a way in and out that was so well hidden on the outside that neither of them detected it. She thought of the garage level.

Even though the roof appeared to be completely collapsed over the garage, what if there was space to wiggle in and out?

She grinned, relieved that she wasn't going to have to figure out a way to scurry back up through the ceiling onto the fourth floor. Terri raided the living room, busting open electronics and removing metal components and even taking some decorations from the walls.

A pungent scent wafted through the lower level of the house. Until that moment, the scent had been contained in the upper levels of the house. Why was it penetrating the main floor now? Saliva filled her mouth as her stomach protested the strong scent of rot. Groaning, Terri slapped a hand over her mouth and nose, trying not to breathe it in.

Fuck, that was awful! How was it even worse than it had been upstairs?

Her eyes flew to the side as she heard a creak from the kitchen, her muscles freezing. Quickly she snuffed out her light, throwing the room into darkness. She'd been an idiot not to connect the dots, but she assumed that no one would have been able to get inside.

She'd been wrong. Very, very wrong.

Terri jumped when a door banged open in the kitchen just off the living room where she stood. Heavy breathing broke the silence. Inhaling through her nose and exhaling through her mouth, she breathed as silently as possible, unwilling to even move in her desperate bid to not be discovered.

A chuckle broke the silence, the pitch sliding unevenly through the laughter, making her skin prickle and the fine hairs on her arms stand on end.

"Little girl," a voice called out, shifting into falsetto as a male voice called out to her. "I know you are here. Come out, sweet little thing. I won't hurt you."

Terri pressed herself against the wall, staring blindly, searching through the darkness.

"Oh, don't be shy. You aren't scared, are you? I wouldn't hurt a sweet girl like you." He paused and giggled. "Ah, you saw *them*, didn't you? A man has to eat, sweet girl, but I wouldn't do more than taste. I would sip you like the sweetest water." He growled and thrashed as he stumbled through the kitchen into the living room.

Terri inched along the wall, her body shivering in fear. *He was insane!* His words fell disjointedly as he spoke to himself almost as much as to her.

"Disgusting, filthy Reapers. They tried to attack me, but *I* made them sorry. I locked them in a room. All but one. Him, I pushed against the wall and gutted right there, devouring his innards while he screamed. It was a precious sound. Not as sweet as your screams will be, my sweet one. No. Not as sweet." His voice quickened with excitement. "I kept the others until I hungered again, and again I took one. They kept me fed for weeks, those nasty Reapers, while they were fed the bloated corpses of their brethren to keep them alive. But they know all about eating people. Can't fault them for doing that. Survival of the fittest, as my father would say."

He darted forward, slamming into the wall just feet away from her, his fingernails scratching along the wood, loudly tearing into the wallpaper as he screamed. "*Where are you?!*"

She bit her tongue, feeling blood well into her mouth with its iron flavor as she tried not to scream in terror. His hands slapped the walls, scratching, pounding, searching for her. Terri took a step toward the kitchen and then another before bolting. She couldn't muffle her steps as she ran terrified through the kitchen, his footsteps pounding as he called out.

"Come back! *Come back! Mine! You are mine!*"

Her heart raced as she rounded a corner. His long fingernails caught on her shirt before she broke free, her blood curdling with his screams of rage. She could hear Veral's furious roar outside, and something heavy began to strike the outside of the building, making the weakened walls tremble from the brute force.

She needed to get out of there! She needed to get to Veral before he brought the entire house down in his attempt to get her free. Twisting to the left, she flew away from the banging, appreciating that the loud noise would confuse the man pursuing her. Knowing that the entrance was blocked, she plunged down the steps into the garage, her breath coming out in loud, uneven pants.

Fingers scraping against the walls, tears sprung to her eyes. It had to be there somewhere. He wasn't getting in without some kind of entrance. Soft wisps brushed her hands and she shuddered, willing herself not to think of the spiders that made dark basements and garages their homes. She gasped involuntarily as he bellowed from the top of the steps. Her fingernails broke low beneath the quick as she dug them between boards until she found one that was loose enough when nudging it that it shifted, spilling sunlight into the room. That was it. On the other side, Terri could hear a loud snarling as something dug and scratched at it.

"*No!*"

"*Fuck you!*" she screamed as she wrenched open the board.

Sunlight spilled in, illuminating the waxen face of her pursuer. He threw his arms up to shield his eyes, but not before she saw the terrible grin pulling unnaturally at his face and the pustules rupturing on his skin. The moment she got the board open, Krono surged in, his massive jaws snapping violently. The whips on his head vibrated and wrapped around his prey, latching tight as his jaws dug in and brought the man to the ground with an inhuman scream.

Unwilling to look back, Terri bolted out into the sunlight, colliding with a huge, muscular form. Black body armor creaked as Veral bent to look down at her, his eyes scanning her with hints of metallic silver in their arctic blue depths. His mandibles expanding fully, he inhaled as he flexed them, and his lips peeled back from his sharp teeth. Spinning around, he plunged into the darkness after Krono. The dorashnal's snarls fell silent and Veral's growl echoed with raw ferocity out to where she stood shivering despite the heat of the afternoon sun.

When the man began to scream, Terri shuddered. When he stopped, she sagged against a wall with relief. Veral came out moments later, Krono by his side. Both of them were heavily splashed with blood, but she welcomed the sight. As he stood over her, chest heaving, covered in the blood of her attacker, Terri stepped forward and wrapped her arms around him. The alien froze in her embrace, but she pressed her face against his upper abs and whispered into his armor.

"Thank you."

His body vibrated, a shudder easing down its length, before two solid arms descended around her and he held her until she stopped shaking.

9

*V*eral held the trembling female in his arms, his teeth bared and his mandibles flaring in a warning to any male who might be watching in the vicinity. He did not pick up on any heat signatures, but he was determined that there be no mistake. He had not picked up the male inside the building until he had moved out of the lower level of the domicile to seek out Terri. The dense stone had blocked his heat signature. Veral had been furious when the male had suddenly turned up on his scan of the building. When the human had dared to threaten her, Veral's anger turned terrible with his inability to find a way to her.

If it hadn't been for Krono discovering the opening…

He shook with rage, a low, threatening hiss escaping between his double tongues. Terri started to wiggle with a muttered protest. Veral pulled back just enough to look down at her curiously.

"What is that?" she muttered. "Something wet is pressing against my arm… oh fuck!"

He watched as her face went pale, her gaze fixed on the trophy hanging from his belt. She scooted back as far as his reach would allow, her face contorting into a grimace. Veral's vibrissae puffed out with pride as he reached down to unfasten the metal trophy catcher from his belt. The hook impaled the severed head of her foe through the base of the skull, erupting through the eye-socket. He gave it a jiggle to make sure it wasn't coming loose.

He frowned. It was secure. That wasn't the source of the problem. His nose wrinkled in disgust at the pustules covering the pale skin and irregular skull formations. "Do not be concerned," he assured her. "I will be certain to have this cleaned and sanitized for you to be a proper trophy in your honor."

"Trophy?" The words left her mouth in a squeak and her throat worked as she continued to stare at it. Veral narrowed his eyes, attempting to work out the problem. He could see none and imagined that she was overwhelmed at the honor done for her.

"It is a privilege to honor you with the head of your enemy," he offered. "You showed admirable skill in evading the male."

"Right." Her lips trembled into an uncertain smile. "Thank you for the honor. You can just hold onto it for right now, if that's all right?"

He nodded and reattached the trophy catcher. His eyes tracked her movements as she continued to shake and glance around nervously. She was not going to be able to function like that. Veral was also now aware that the residents of Phoenix were far more dangerous than he gave them credit for if lone males were attacking outside of the threat that the Reapers posed. He disliked the thought. Males running together he could easily detect from a safe distance away, but the fact that a single male could potentially get through without alerting him pricked at him. It was a slim chance, but enough that his focus narrowed on an insistent, pressing need to prowl the perimeter, looking for signs of males coming too close.

"Enough for today," he said abruptly, nearly surprising himself as much as her with his quick decision. Still, it was a sound idea. "I need to tend to the trophy while it is still fresh, and you are of no use to me while you are on edge."

He paused and huffed as he took a look around the quiet street, his eyes narrowing suspiciously. He had not anticipated any threat coming from that quarter and had been lax and dismissive.

He would not make the same mistake.

"We will resume tomorrow."

Terri peered up at him curiously but slowly nodded her head without questioning him. A hot flash of approval shot through him at her submission to his authority. Although Terri was undeniably spirited and possessed a hard will, she surrendered to him in a way that he demanded... and even craved. With a command to Krono, he trailed after her down the street. Though he kept her within his sight, much of his attention was also trained on their surroundings as they made their way down the empty street.

A frustrated growl rattled in his chest as his eyes rested on her once again for longer and more frequently than necessary. He tilted his head in confusion as he watched the delicate female sway in front of him with every step she took. He considered that perhaps he was malfunctioning. He had never concerned himself much with the females of his own kind, much less been inclined to protect a female of another species. Though he honored her as was right, he shouldn't be so fascinated with the human. He ran his diagnostics check as he continued to follow behind at a reasonable pace. He frowned as all his systems checked back fully operational.

Was he developing an attachment? The idea filled him with a certain amount of horror and an undeniable curiosity. He fisted his hands, his retractable claws sliding out into his palm with a sharp sting of pain. A welcome distraction. He pulled his gaze off her and returned it to their surroundings as they traveled for some distance. As it happened, he had been a little too effective in forcing his attention away from her, and hadn't noticed that she stopped until he nearly ran into her after a rapid flash of light he caught on the edges of his vision.

Her soft body collided with his and Veral held back a snarl when a strange need whipped through him, far too quickly for him to identify before it was gone. All he knew was that it left him achy and bewildered. His nanos flooded his system in confusion, trying to correct whatever undeterminable error he experienced as he tried to make sense of what had happened.

His awareness shifted to the female in front of him and he became immediately aware of her reason for stopping. He stiffened as thunder rumbled in the distance, accompanied by another flash of lightning. His vibrissae lifted out away from him warily. Storms on Argurumal were treacherous. If Terri's expression was anything to go by, they weren't to be treated lightly here either. Krono stood on a pile of rock from a crumpled wall a short distance ahead of him, his vibrissae whipping around him in the air seconds before the dorashnal howled.

Terri shivered and crouched, pulling her pack off her shoulder as another crash of thunder sounded in the distance. The sound was followed by yet another. Her face scrunched up as she peered back at him, digging into her bag. A sharp wind blew through, stinging them with sand, and in the near distance, a wall of sand began to shift into the air at a concerning rate.

"Storm coming," she stated loudly over the noise as she pulled a cloth hanging loose at her neck over her face. "Good thing we decided to go in. The sandstorms around here are no joke! I don't think we have much farther to travel."

Squinting at the street, he verified the accuracy of her estimation. Even with the storm moving in quickly, they would reach their camp destination soon.

Lowering his inner eyelids to protect them from the windblown sand, Veral took position standing over her protectively, his back against the stinging bite of the wind as she dug for whatever she was searching for. With a triumphant snarl, she pulled out a pair of bulky, worn goggles, snapping them on over her eyes just in time before the wall of sand hit them. The wind shrieked around them, muffling everything. Terri raised her voice to be heard over the wind, though he could have heard her just fine at a lower volume. She tapped her goggles with one hand for emphasis as she spoke.

"I found these a few years back at an abandoned airfield." She tilted her head and peered at his placid expression. "How is it that your eyes aren't bothering you?"

He leaned in close, a finger raised to his eye so that her attention was drawn to it, before briefly drawing his inner lid to the side. She flinched, her breath drawing in on a quick gasp as it slammed shut once more to protect his eyes from the grit.

"My species is accustomed to such an environment and are adapted to it. Far better than humans, it seems."

Her lips part in another human grin. "Guess so."

The goggles darkened her eyes so that he was unable to see them any longer. He did not like that they concealed her eyes in such a fashion. Not only that, but they were inferior and fit her face oddly so that tiny granules of sand were still creeping in. They were clearly meant for a male. He frowned at the ill construction. It was a decent substitute for a species that didn't have an inner protective eyelid, though he imagined he could fashion her something more efficient in his ship. When they took their first load back, he would look among his scrap materials to craft something appropriate for her.

Without saying anything else, Terri swung her pack on her shoulders and turned away from him to head down the street once more. Krono jogged after her, his six feet picking up with swift steps as his head lowered against the wind. Veral watched them, clicking his mandibles thoughtfully. Giving his head an abrupt, aggressive shake, his vibrissae rattling in agitation, he spared a glance to make sure the collector carts were rolling after them as his wide, stalking steps easily kept pace.

When they squeezed into their sleeping chamber—the outer room being inundated with sand—and the door firmly shut behind them, Veral snarled and shook the sand off himself. Even Krono seemed to stumble to a corner where he settled on a pile of rags that Terri had gathered for him to serve as a bed. Walking against a storm was a lot of work even for Argurma, so he was not surprised when the female bent over, her weight braced on her hands against her thighs.

After several minutes, Terri recovered enough to laugh before sidling up to a large wooden case. Throwing her weight against it, Veral watched as it slid painfully slow across the floor, moving in the direction of the door to barricade it against the storm. Growling, Veral stepped by her, nudging her aside as he lifted it and moved it effortlessly. As he set it down in front of the door, he could feel her eyes on him while she swiped her hands over her arms and shoulders before dropping her bag in the center of the room. Terri peeled her goggles off and grinned up at him cheerfully. Despite the goggles protecting her eyes, her face and arms were red from where the sand had rubbed her raw before they made it inside.

"Well, that's that. At least we don't have to worry about the Reapers for the next couple of nights. They won't be out in this mess either. That's about the only good thing about a sandstorm. Nothing, and no one, goes out."

Bending over, her ass jutted in the air as she picked up her bag and overturned it. Pieces of metal chinked and whispered against each other, though a dull impact of something larger hitting the sand drew his attention. He crouched down to look at it just as Terri snatched it up from the sand. He turned his scope light from his wrist comm on it and frowned to see a simple wooden box.

"Oh, don't scowl," Terri muttered, her nose wrinkling at him as if with distaste though her eyes were lit with humor. "This is something wonderful. I had one as a child and I couldn't pass it up. Watch."

She set it on her lap as she knelt on the floor. The fingers of one hand drifted to the back to wind a small metal key several turns. Flashing him a smile, she lifted the lid on the box, and inside a delicate figure of a female spun around as a melody of some kind sang out from it. He raised his eyes to Terri and found her humming along to the melody, her eyes closed as she swayed with the music. Though the low light obscured much of her body outside of what was provided by the limited light of his scope, the pleasure on her face and the way she moved was so ethereal that everything within him paused to give undivided attention to her. His mandibles clicked and he trilled.

Slowly, her pale eyes opened, and she looked at him. Beads of moisture clung to her eyelashes, which she hurried to wipe away with the back of her wrist. He leaned in close, his heavy brow lowering. His mandibles expanded and he inhaled. There was a hint of sadness, but something else that confused him.

"Why are you leaking?" he demanded brusquely.

Soft laughter rolled from her lips that intrigued him and made something within him tighten with interest.

"I'm just a little teary. Playing this reminded me of some good memories. I recognized the melody." Her voice softened as she sang nonsense words of a peculiar place that existed over a rainbow that brought happiness. He scowled.

"That makes no sense. Rainbows are from the sun catching moisture as they reflect a prism of light. There is nothing on the other side of a rainbow except more air. Nothing can be gained of significant value from that."

Her lips thinned at him. "Rain can bring hope, yeah? So when it rains and water in the sky after the rain makes a rainbow shine, it can represent happiness with that hope, can it not?" she challenged.

He tilted his head in consideration. "Your logic is strange. Hope is unreliable, and yet I cannot dispute that you *may* have a point."

Just that quickly, her expression evened out and her lips quirked once more. "I just may get you to believe in magic yet," she teased.

He flared his vibrissae in mock irritation. "Do not test me female. I have no interest in such silliness." His regard, however, softened toward her as she began to hum once more little dreams that were perhaps long forgotten within him along with everything else.

erri sang to herself as she wetted a rag. She sat naked on a blanket facing away from Veral. Normally she might have felt unease with a male in the room, but she trusted him, especially after several occasions when she'd changed clothes at night with him in the room without any reaction. It made it easier that he didn't have any sexual interest in her.

That kind of stung too, since she had recently found her eyes tracking him more frequently, admiring his tall, strong build. His features had taken some time to become accustomed to, but after a few days, she found them more interesting than intimidating. Usually. Sometimes he still did things that gave her a pause. Like the so-called trophy he'd stripped off his belt as he was carefully burning away excess flesh with a small handheld laser.

Turning her attention back to her bathing, Terri tried to ignore it. Normally she wouldn't waste any of her collected water, but after brushing up against the severed head followed by battling through a sandstorm, her skin itched and crawled until she gave in and decided to use a sparing amount of her precious water on a sponge bath.

Dragging the wet cloth over her breasts, she paused, her skin tingling as she felt Veral's gaze on her back. He rumbled out a low growl, but that was all before the weight of his gaze slid away, much to her secret disappointment. Swallowing, she made quick work of washing the rest of her body, slicking the cloth between her thighs only once before shimmying into an old threadbare nightshirt.

Embarrassed at the direction of her thoughts, she avoided looking at him as she climbed into the pile of blankets that served as her own bed. It was insane to entertain such interest. He was a fucking alien! Their anatomy probably wasn't even compatible. Her cheeks heated at the thought as she burrowed down into her bedding.

Settling down into the warmth of the blankets in the chill desert night air, her eyes began to drift closed only to snap open when Veral got up and strode over to the discarded cloth. She kept her eyelids lowered, watching him from beneath her lashes as he bent and picked up the cloth. Her breath caught as he turned it in his hand.

He must have wanted to bathe too. She should have thought to offer.

He did not, however, reach immediately for the water bottle. He stared down at the cloth, clicking his mandibles quietly to himself before rubbing the damp, used cloth across his chest. His bare chest! Her eyes flung wide open. She'd never seen him without his body armor. He was stripped down to a simple cloth barely covering his groin. Was that how he always slept? She wouldn't know. Veral was always dressed when she went to bed, keeping watch late into the night beyond her own endurance as he seemed to require less sleep than her.

Her breath escaped her in a shudder as he swiped the cloth over his face several times before trailing it back down to his chest and finally dipping the cloth to his groin. The male growled, his eyes seeking hers out in the low light of the fire he'd built in the center of the room shortly after their return. He watched her, the whip tendrils on his head puffing out around him, writhing as they made a soft swishing sound. Desire surged through her, heating her belly, dampening her pussy and upper thighs despite her best efforts to resist it. Terri shivered as his mandibles widened and his lips parted as if he were tasting the air. A low, aggressive growl filled the room.

It was frightening and exhilarating, making her lust spike in a way that didn't seem entirely healthy to her. What sort of person lusted over another making such sounds? Apparently, she did. No matter how much she tried to control or ignore it, it surged through her unpredictably and with such strength that she was caught help-less in it until it eased. It never truly passed, for even after the brunt of it was gone, that edge and awareness remained, taunting her.

Veral's growl gradually became louder, responding to her rising need. She observed that his whips had not only puffed out but were moving around his head as if in a seeking motion. He took a step toward her and her belly clenched in anticipation. Suddenly, his mandibles snapped closed and he shook his head before step-ping away from her. Going to the door, he pushed the barrier away just enough to allow him to slip out. Then he was gone.

Terri's face stained crimson as she ducked into the blankets. He probably thought she was going to jump him or something in a burst of uncontrollable lust. The snort turned into a giggle as she tried to imagine herself doing just that, given that he had consider-ably more height and weight than her. Her humor died away at the memory of the way he shook himself as if touched by something unpleasant.

No, she was going to have to do better at controlling herself if she wanted to hang around long enough to catch that ride. Still, the sting of rejection was a painful reminder of just how alone she was.

That was fine. She *liked* being alone. No one tried to control her, and she didn't have to answer to anyone except herself. She never had to censor her thoughts when she talked aloud to herself

—one of the unfortunate consequences of her isolation. She knew that she had no filter and often caught herself rambling about anything and everything to Veral's silent silhouette at her side. Really, his presence wasn't much different than having a pet.

She sighed. A pet would be welcome. She doubted that Veral would part with Krono but maybe she could find something among human settlements once she got to the coast.

That was all she needed. That she was happier than she'd been in a while had nothing to do with the surly male.

Having Veral around was messing with her hormones. The irony was not lost upon her that her biological clock ticked a bit too loudly for a male that likely wasn't even compatible with her. She laughed at herself. That figured. Of course it couldn't be a handsome human passing through who would sweep her away. No, she was drawn to a male who not only came from literally an entirely different planet but who also had so much technology implanted in him that his responses were often much more cold and calculating than what she'd consider normal.

That whole thing with the head had been bizarre too. Her lips quirked slightly at how proud he'd looked as he explained that it was a trophy specifically to honor her. That was almost sweet—if she could get beyond the fact that it had been a decapitated human head. Settling back to her normal routine, with fewer severed heads, would be welcome.

Terri stared into the dark and sighed, her eyes straining in the low light of the fire. Who was she kidding? She hated it. Her life before Veral came—having no one but herself to speak with day in and day out unless she ran into Meg, and even then she had to hurry before they were caught—had been one of barely existing. Veral gave her something she hadn't had since her father died: someone to connect to and lean on. Not that she would say so to him. No doubt he would deliver a caustic reply before directing his attention to something else that required it. She wondered what he would think if he knew that she'd miss him when they finally went their own ways.

That led to another troubling thought. Once she was on the coast, then what?

Terri shifted anxiously beneath her blanket, drawing Krono's attention to her. The dorashnal made a whining-trilling noise and squirmed over to her side. Terri opened her arms gratefully as he snuggled against her torso, his massive length curling around her as he pressed against her. As they lay side-by-side, his whips affectionately stroked her skin and patted her. Sighing, her arms wound around his thick neck and hugged him tight. The contact alone was soothing and became even more so when he began to purr contently like a giant cat. She brushed the tip of her nose against the top of his head in a loving nuzzle. His whips moved to caress her face. It did little to diminish her frustrated arousal, but it at least soothed her until she finally fell asleep.

It was sometime later when she awoke to the sound of the door swinging open and bumping against the dresser. Terri watched from behind Krono's massive shoulder as Veral growled at it and pushed it open to step inside before maneuvering it back into place. His eyes brushed her briefly, but he strode by, barely acknowledging her presence as he grabbed his bedding and pulled it clear to the farthest corner of the room. Terri frowned but concealed her expression against Krono's neck, her eyes shut tight against the sight of him preparing for bed. She hadn't expected him to lay beside her and hold her again tonight, but that he felt it necessary to move clear across the room, farther away than he'd ever lain before, pissed her off.

As if being near her were contaminating him in some fashion, or maybe that he didn't trust her to control her lust. She rolled her eyes with a small sneer.

What a dick.

Rolling over, she gave him her back as she pressed her lower back and bottom against Krono's warm side. He immediately shifted to snuggle around her once more and lay his head across her neck. Determined to ignore the asshole on the other side of the room, she sighed happily from the way Krono's body heat seeped into her muscles. Tightening her thighs to provide some relief to her sex, she drew her blanket up and dismissed the infuriating male from her thoughts.

11

*T*he second day of the sandstorm wasn't any better than the first for Veral. His skin itched and tingled all over and it had nothing to do with the sand finding its way into their shelter. Several times, he left to get some reprieve from Terri's intoxicating scent that was causing strange chemical reactions that his nanos were working overtime to neutralize. Was he having a bad reaction to her pheromones? He typically didn't spend much time in the presence of other species outside of delivering instructions for the salvage teams following in his wake. Perhaps an allergy to her pheromones was the cause. He didn't believe that it could be his mating heat.

In all his revolutions away from Argurumal, he'd never once had more than the vaguest of responses to any female from his civix. He glanced over at Terri and was relieved to find her distracted by Krono with her back to him. While her attention was diverted, he pulled open his pants and inspected his civix pouch. As expected, it was still unbroken, the seam still fused. He poked at it gently with one claw. Did it look a bit thin in some spots? He analyzed the area and found it to be an eighth of a millimeter thinner than it had been. He growled and sealed his pants once more. It was possible, if he was having a reaction to her pheromones, that the moderate swelling of his civix alone would have caused the weakening.

As long as he wasn't extruding, everything was fine. Uncomfortable but still within the limits of the laws. While he preferred to remain separate from Argurumal, he didn't wish to be hunted for violating any of the planetary laws. He knew with the link between his systems and his brethren that someone would notice if he extruded and went into the consequential mating heat.

His eyes drifted back over to Terri and he grimaced. He could admit that he was fascinated with the female. She had so much strength within her delicate, vulnerable body. It made him hunger for it.

He hadn't been untruthful when he told her that many males would have courted her as a worthy mate if she'd been Argurma. Even as a human, she still wouldn't suffer any lack of males vying for her attention, but it would have happened only after she'd received basic control implants and permission was granted from the mating registrar. They would insist on the implants to tie her to Argurumal, whereas mating would do nothing more than load her system with nanos, extending her life and linking it to that of her mate without interfering with her mind or autonomy. He could almost imagine the pleasure that would come with being tied to her… Though he saw what it did to his sire, a part of him drew toward her, seeking to bind to her with his vibrissae.

Terri looked over her shoulder at him and his body tensed, uncertain if she was going to approach and surround him in the overwhelming pull of her pheromones. She didn't move; instead, she turned away and bared her teeth in a smile at Krono, who took it as permission to drape his massive frame over her lap while she bent down to smother him in affection. Veral felt his vibrissae lift away from him into the air as jealousy speared through him. He drew them back down with self-admonishment. He was acting absurd over the affection that the female was giving his dorashnal.

It was illogical for Veral to possess any sort of feeling toward the human female, or to even consider that she might set off his mating heat. He was on Earth for a limited time, and despite her fears, the female was capable of taking care of herself. She would relocate to a better area with his aid, as promised, and perhaps take a mate and attempt to breed a new generation of humans. It was the logical outcome... so why did he want to kill something so badly? Not just something. He lusted to destroy *any* male who would so much as even attempt to touch Terri.

Maybe he would even procure a dorashnal pup and have it delivered to her to give her company and added protection. He would protect her from the unwanted advances of males, even if he had to acknowledge that she would eventually find a mate. Until then, however, she would be safe. Even a pup was dangerous to most beings after it bonded. Given the way that Krono was acting like a lovesick pup over the female, he had no doubt that one would bond to her.

He could clearly read the dorashnal's frustration as Krono rolled against her, his vibrissae tapping against her. He was instinctively trying to lure out her dorashnal that she would also have had if she'd been born Argurma. Such signaling could prompt a mating between dorashnals that could disastrously provoke the mating heat between a male and female Argurma if they weren't careful. At least that was something Veral didn't have to worry about with Terri, though Krono didn't understand why a female wasn't presenting herself to him for mating. Veral growled and looked away.

It was for the best.

With a growl, he pushed himself to his feet. He couldn't stay still any longer. He would do a circuit to check his traps. Even though he could go several days without food, he knew that Terri couldn't. In any case, he desired the distraction that it offered. "I will be back," he rumbled. In a few short steps, he was at the door and pushing the barrier out of the way again. He could feel the female's eyes on him, but she said nothing.

Veral stepped out into the hallway and immediately closed his inner eyelids as a gust of sand blew over him. He stood rooted in place, his mind still occupied with Terri. Her behavior had been strange since yesterday. Usually, the female filled the space around him with her voice, especially when they were at rest, but something had changed. Although he found it annoying at first, he hadn't realized how accustomed he'd become to it until she lapsed into silence. He narrowed his eyes at the door. What had transpired while he was away? He hadn't been gone long, only enough to escape the overwhelming pull of her pheromones, but when he returned, she'd refused to acknowledge him. Instead, she remained curled up with Krono while the wind howled outside.

Clicking his mandibles in irritation, he made his way into the exposed main room and stepped out into the street. Though the air around him bore a reddish-yellow tinge from the sand, he had little trouble seeing through the thin membrane of his inner eyelid. Even his nostrils sealed with a porous membrane. He was able to breathe adequately enough, and it kept the sand out, although it did so at the sacrifice of his sense of smell. He could always open his mandibles and mouth to taste the air if necessary, though it would result in a mouth full of sand which would be entirely unpleasant. As an extra precaution, he pulled up the folds of material at the neck of his armor until it covered his nose, mouth, and mandibles.

Standing in the center of the empty street, Veral's eyes scanned the distance, his sensors kicking on to analyze everything before him. He increased the scope of his vision and smiled grimly. As Terri had said, there were no humans risking the sandstorm. Snapping his vibrissae, Veral headed down the street to the first of his traps, his feet taking him farther away from Terri once again. Just as when he'd left her before, his body tightened and protested. Every nerve screamed in agony, yet this time the sensation was more acute. So was the unease that filled him. Although he knew that she was safe in the dwelling while the sands blew, the greater the distance between them, the stronger his discomfort grew.

A roar of helpless rage ripped out of him as he threw his head back, protesting to the uncaring heavens of the universe. He did not want to believe it, but all signs pointed to the fact that he was bonding to the human female. He wanted to return to his ship and leave Earth with what little salvage he acquired. He even went as far as turning in the direction of his ship and heading in that direction, determined to seek out safety in space, far away from the dying planet.

He did not get far before his feet stopped, unwilling to go any farther than the edge of the city limits.

He peered at the shadowy form of the red rocks jutting into the sky in the distance. No matter how he willed it, his processors refused to respond, and his body remained rooted to the spot, unwilling to get any farther from Terri. The bond had already advanced beyond the point of no return. There was no way he could flee or sever it. All that remained was the final step. Once he extruded, he would be powerless to prevent his instinct from taking over to seed the female. At that point, the bond would be complete and the officials on Argurumal would be alerted to his deviance. He would have little choice but to take the human and move farther into uncharted space.

He shook his head, whipping his vibrissae with the force of his movement. It was a good thing that he was an independent salvager. His contracts would not be dependent on the favor of Argurumal. Given that his homeworld made no efforts to maintain alliances with other civilizations in the sectors, they would not be able to interfere with his operations. They would, however, send elite teams of Argurma hunters to capture him and his mate.

He would be dragging the female into danger. The thought did not appeal to him.

He debated if it would be kinder to kill her and spare her the future that would now lie ahead of them. He would suffer endlessly from her absence, but she wouldn't suffer. Humans were small and fragile. He could hold her in his arms, and imprint to his databanks the final memories he'd have of her before snapping her neck effortlessly with one hand. He could do it before the bond became any stronger.

Even as he envisioned it, Veral knew he would be incapable of carrying it out, even to spare her. He groaned and sat on a rock as he stared out into the swirling sands. His decision came to him quickly. He would resist the call of her pheromones and his instincts for as long as he could to give them more time to collect what they needed. A full cargo would get them a lot further. There was a repository just within Federation space where he could deposit the goods to be collected. From there, it would just be a matter of waiting for the credits to appear. He would continue to weave back and forth over the border, exploring new worlds to salvage and returning to resupply. If they were fortunate, they would be able to stay out of the grip of the Argurumal council for many revolutions, if not most of their long lives.

He found the idea of spending hundreds of revolutions with Terri more appealing than he would have anticipated. He chuffed and shook his head again. He wouldn't have hundreds of revolutions if he did not keep her fed. Veral headed back into the city, tracking the coordinates for the nearest of his traps.

To his frustration, the first trap was empty, as were the second and third. The fourth trap had a long legless creature that coiled up at his approach, its black tongue flicking out at him as the end of its tail shook sending up a sound not unlike his vibrissae. He recognized the warning and bared his teeth at it. With one swift motion, he drew out his taka blade, the same which had gained him the trophy for Terri, and pierced the top of the creature's skull, splitting its head from its body within the span of half a breath. Yanking his blade free from where it was buried in the earth beneath the creature, he sent the electrical charge over it, cleansing the length of it while he snatched up the creature with the other hand. He ruffled his vibrissae while giving the creature's head a passing glance.

It had not been a great enough foe to keep as a trophy. He wondered if the planet had any beasts yet that might present a suitable challenge. He made quick work of stripping the internal organs from the creature. As he dropped it into a dark, expandable sack on his belt, he acknowledged that it was perhaps foolish to wish for such a thing. There was enough distraction from his work, with the Reapers being an unpleasant nuisance and a mate bonding lighting his blood on fire. A hunt challenge would be best pursued later when he could afford the indulgence. He would look forward to that day. It had been some time since he enjoyed a hunt. Idly, he wondered if he shouldn't just hunt the Reapers and take his pleasure.

No. His work required his attention first.

Nothing would prevent him from taking his pleasure reaping *them*, the same way they threaten to do among their own kind, after his tasks were satisfied.

He bared his teeth once more as he navigated among the buildings, locking on to the coordinates of the domicile where he left Terri. As he returned to his camp, he found that his spirits were surprisingly high as he drew near. He suspected that it was largely the release of chemicals into his blood and brain at the instinctual satisfaction of nearing his bonded female once more. His body, which had been stressed the entire time they were apart, was reacting in a way that he at least understood.

Terri glanced up at him from her spot, her brows jerking up. Tilting her head to the side she regarded him curiously. "You seem happy," she observed.

He bared his teeth triumphantly as he produced the legless earth-slider from the bag at his side. "One of the traps yielded a positive result. I shall feed you now."

"I can't say I've ever eaten snake before," she admitted with a tiny twist of her lips.

He glanced down at it uncertainly. "My scans indicate that the meat is safe to eat. Do you find it objectionable?"

She shook her head, her smile growing. "No, I've just never met anyone who would hunt a large rattlesnake like that. They're aggressive and fast."

Veral snorted, his vibrissae shaking in amusement. "And I am not?"

A laugh trilled out of her and her eyes sparkled with humor.

"Good point," she acknowledged. "All right, let's skewer the sucker. I'm starving."

He paused, his head snapping to her with concern. "You are starving. You did not say that your condition was so deplorable. I would have fed you earlier."

Terri stared at him for a heartbeat and then laughed once more. "No. No. I'm sorry. It's an expression. An exaggeration. I'm just really hungry and looking forward to eating."

Slowly, his lips curved in understanding, and he bent down to retrieve the elongated emergency pin from his supplies that had served in cooking their meat over the open fire. It threaded through the creature—the snake, she called it—and he set it over the flames. As it cooked, a melody drifted through his mind in his mother's voice. He leaned forward, trilling and humming the tune as he carefully watched and rotated the meat, all too aware of his female's eyes on him.

His female. Veral's vibrissae puffed up in pleasure. Somehow, he already liked the sound of it.

*A*lthough she tried to put distance between herself and Veral, Terri found it difficult and gave up on it completely after he returned with dinner. She knew that he didn't need to eat as often as she did, for he had been surprised by her admission of just how often she required sustenance the first day they were together. That he went out into the sandstorm to provide for her was sweet, and the wall she'd erected between them crumbled all too easily.

So much for any sense of self-preservation.

Terri watched him curiously as she ate. Unlike a human, Veral seemed to not be disturbed at all or even really notice the distance. She bit back a smile and stuffed more food into her mouth. He probably considered it another human eccentricity that was tolerable regardless of whether or not it was considered rude in his culture. She couldn't help but stare. He was crouched beside her, close enough that she could reach out and touch the bunched muscles of his thigh.

It was a far cry from his earlier behavior. In fact, he was carefully stripping meat and handing her one bite-sized morsel at a time. He ate as well, but he was so attentive to her needs that she wondered what provoked the shift in his disposition toward her when earlier he was making every effort to stay as far away from her as possible.

"All right, what gives?" she asked abruptly and then winced at her lack of tact. He was being nice to her and she was accusing him of an ulterior motive.

One horned brow lifted. "Gives what?"

Terri huffed. "I mean—I've noticed you've been trying to stay as far away from me as possible, like I had a disease you were concerned over catching. So why are you being nice to me and coming near me again?"

He tilted his head. "Is this the reason you were silent and not speaking ceaselessly in your normal habit?"

She flushed at the observation. She knew she had what her father laughingly called verbal diarrhea, without even the grace of a mental filter to save anyone in her company from hearing anything at all that sprang to her mind. Maybe she had chattered too much at the alien over the days if he found her silence *that* unusual.

"I didn't think there was anything worth saying if you didn't want to be around me. I was *trying* to be considerate," she muttered.

His arctic and silver eyes narrowed on her. "You were insulted and reacting with anger," he corrected. She felt her face getting hotter but shrugged in a manner that she hoped appeared to be nonchalant. Veral chuffed knowingly, adding to her humiliation. Terri thought of moving away from him when a thick arm banded in front of her, stopping all movement as he held her in place. He leaned in against her, his head lowered, and Veral's blunt, broad nose trailed along her jaw in a manner that made her belly clench with desire at the hot fan of breath over her skin. He nuzzled her as his lips dropped down to her ear.

"I *was* trying to escape you," he hissed softly in her ear. "Your presence is overwhelming to my systems. The delectable scent of your pheromones, your inquisitiveness, your spirit, even the sound of your voice..." he whispered and brushed his nose against the rim of her ear. A shiver ran down her spine. "I thought to escape you, but there is no escape. I couldn't even leave the city before my processors refused to cooperate. My systems will not allow me to part from you now. You have awakened something in me that should have been left to sleep, little human, and now you will have to suffer the consequences."

"What consequences?" she rasped. She was proud of herself for getting the words out. Her tongue wasn't following directions and her entire body tingled with awareness. She tried to keep from panting and prayed that he didn't notice the way moisture was slipping out from between her thighs on the wave of arousal crashing over her.

Veral drew away, his thick lips nipping at her ear with only the slightest sting of his teeth. The feeling shot straight down to her clit and her hips jerked in reaction. One large hand pressed on her pelvis, capturing her and dragging her against his body as he held her still. "Not yet," he growled huskily, his voice low and intimate. He nuzzled the nape of her neck and a breath panted out of him.

"Your smell…" He groaned. "It has changed. My oath, it is beyond anything I've experienced. My systems crave and seek it."

Her breath came out in ragged pants. "You're smelling my arousal. It's my body's response to everything you are doing to me. It is… a natural reaction."

Veral surged to his feet, dropping Terri so quickly that she fell backward. Brushing her hair out of her face, she watched him in confusion while he growled and paced. The whips around his head twitched wildly, rattling impotently as he walked the length of the room repeatedly back and forth. With considerable effort, she reined in her desire as she looked up at him with concern.

"Are you okay? Your whips are going wild there," she said quietly.

He shot her a confused look. "Whips?"

"Yeah, you know—hanging from your head," she motioned with her hands over her hair in a demonstration. He peered at her with amusement and chuffed, his anxiety forgotten, which cheered her considerably, as the long, thin appendages lifted from around his shoulders.

"Are you referring to my vibrissae?" he inquired, his eyes pinning her even as they gleamed with humor.

"Uh, yeah... I guess so," she agreed with a wide grin. "Vibrissae. Well, in my defense, the name I came up with was completely descriptive due to the way they whip around under their own power. I guess I could have gone with calling them head-tentacles."

He immediately gave her a pained look. The appendages flattened against his head. "I am grateful that you do not refer to them in such a way. They are *not* tentacles. My vibrissae are both a secondary defense for my species as well as containing tiny, invisible receptors that helps me gather additional information from my environment for my processors to analyze."

Terri smiled impishly at him before sobering. He seemed in control of himself. Now seemed like a good time to ask him what he'd meant.

"You said that you had to wait... not yet, specifically... what exactly are you talking about?"

Veral fixed her with a vexed look but rolled his neck, his vibrissae—she enjoyed the word—puffing out and twitching around him with the motion. "This situation is without precedent, as far as I am aware, among the Argurma. We take great pains to not bond outside of our species, and yet it seems that my biology has begun the process in reaction to my prolonged contact with you and my own interest and unfortunate sentimentality where you are concerned," he admitted gruffly. "As I indicated, it has advanced to the point where my processors are constantly fixed on you and my systems do not allow me to exceed a distance more than several spans from your side. Even my nanos are coding to the bond, which causes me distress if separated."

"Holy shit," she whispered in awe. She still wasn't sure what all was entailed in this bond he mentioned, but it obviously had a huge impact on his physiology. Enough to where he was understandably concerned.

"Human colloquialisms never fail to confuse me," he muttered.

Terri waved a dismissing hand. "Never mind. Basically, I'm this enormous distraction for you... mostly because this bonding thing is something you cannot control."

His lips tightened but he did not deny it. "You simplify matters too much. You do not understand."

"Okay," she drawled. "So, break it down for me then."

"It is more than an inconvenience. An inconvenience can be dealt with and discarded. Mate bonding is a natural imperative for my kind. Once it begins, we are unable to resist the pull of our mate to complete the bond, regardless of whether those are made outside of appropriate and sanctioned methods."

Her mind breezed over much of what he said, latching onto one word. "Mate. We're... mates?" The concept was surprising but also inspired a warm feeling. She scooted forward suddenly emboldened to try everything she'd been fantasizing about over the last two days. She reached for him. "Then it is okay to touch..."

The good feeling dissipated when his hand closed around her wrist, holding her arm well away from him as he shook his head.

"Not yet," he growled. "I shall avoid solidifying the bond."

Her face crumbled, embarrassed that she misread him to such a degree. She attempted to pull back her hand, but his fingers held fast, not relinquishing it. She glared and tugged harder.

"Veral, let go," she said.

"You misunderstand and are angry again," he retorted.

Her cheeks flamed. "Look, I get it, okay. This bonding thing is not something you want. I totally get it."

A rattling sigh slipped out of him and his fingers caught her chin, pushing until she was forced to meet his eyes.

"It is too dangerous to solidify the bond." She blinked. Was she imagining things or was she hearing a tinge of regret in his words? "Because of that, I have deemed it to be a foolish risk to take. I am responsible for your wellbeing and refuse to put you in the way of harm."

His fingers slipped away from her jaw and he set her free.

Nodding to her blankets, he gave her a meaningful look. "I am certain that we will be outside of the storm tomorrow. Rest, anastha. We have much work to do to make up for lost time."

Confused, Terri watched him as he dropped to the floor a short distance away. She didn't even move when he picked up a weapon and began to treat the blades as he did every night. When it became apparent that he was done discussing the subject, she moved out of the way. Walking over to a wall, she slid to the floor and leaned against it as she watched him.

It seemed that even when it came to a sure thing like mating that she still couldn't win. Terri allowed her head to loll back as she closed her eyes. Of course he was going to just make a decision for them without input from her when it came to her own safety. What if she were willing to risk the danger? The brief tastes of passion and tenderness that she'd received from him were worth it to her. She hungered for such contact and affection. In her mind, it was worth walking a bit on the wild side.

And just how much and what kind of danger was he speaking of? He made it sound almost criminal if he attempted to mate with a female from another species without registered approval. Granted, she didn't know all the details, but how hard would it be to tell her and allow her to come to a decision about how much risk she was willing to take rather than have the big, gruff alien decide on her behalf?

If it were dangerous for her, it could be dangerous for him too. Terri frowned. Sometimes she sounded like a real bitch inside her own head. Although he put the focus on her, she couldn't demand that he ignore the risks when it could likely carry some very severe consequences with it. He had demonstrated without a doubt that he was attracted to her, and how much he needed her, despite his refusal to go further with it. His insistence that they wait was still as cryptic as ever.

If he wasn't going to go through with it, what exactly was he waiting for?

Her eyes never straying far from him, Terri decided to stop

mooning over him and do something productive. Digging through her things, she found her needle and thread. She yanked off her shirt and went to work sewing yet another worn seam back together with slow, neat stitches. She could feel his hot gaze upon her, and she swallowed back a groan, her hands trembling for a moment before she wrestled control back into her grip. Turning the shirt in her lap, she tackled a tear where the shirt had become caught on a fence she hopped earlier.

She flushed and fidgeted as it became apparent that he wasn't going to look away.

"You're staring," she finally said crossly.

Veral grunted. "You are displaying yourself," he muttered. "It is difficult not to look. I am still a male, and a male in the presence of his bonded female. I am not wholly a machine and am a long way from dead."

Pleasure rushed through her.

"Well… I suppose that's different," she agreed magnanimously. "That just leaves me with one question…" She looked up and met his eyes. "Are you enjoying the view?"

His vibrissae fluffed out with a rattling snap, his eyes heating like the blue fire at the heart of a flame. "Indescribably so."

With that, he turned his attention back to his task, and Terri felt a satisfied grin stretch over her face as she focused on her mending. That response was at least promising!

our days later, Veral knew his control was about to snap. Terri was not deliberately provoking him or inciting his desire, but it seemed everything she did made his civix swell. His body shivered with an awareness that it would not be much longer before his mating pouch ruptured, freeing his civix. He tried not to look at his female as he walked across the desert, making certain to keep his pace reasonable so as not to inadvertently leave Terri behind. Unfortunately, he was aware every second of her at his side, her hips swinging in a natural rhythm as they walked over sand, rock, and packed, dry earth as they led the collector carts to the ship. Veral wished that he could have left her in the relative safety of their dwelling with Krono, but since becoming aware of the limits of their bond, he knew that would be impossible. The dorashnal meanwhile leaped over obstacles as his sharp nose reacquainted him with the terrain leading back to the ship. Both his human and Krono were in high spirits as they traversed with him.

Unable to resist, he glanced over at her. Though her face was flushed bright red from the sun beating down on them and the physical exertion from their long walk, her smile was bright, thrilled with the adventure of seeing his ship. She was never more indescribably desirable to him. He wanted to drop her down onto the sand, strip off her clothing, and feast upon her until his civix burst free to set him off on his mating heat. It was a long walk to the ship, long enough that they wouldn't be able to return to camp tonight. A prickle of dread raced over his hide. Would he be able to keep tight control over his desires when she was in his ship, sleeping in his personal space, scenting his possessions and everything within it with her sweet, alluring fragrance? He expanded his mandibles, catching a taste of her salty musk, and his civix twitched roughly.

He was never going to last.

Sooner or later his instinct, paired with the demands of his systems, would override all his intentions. It had been a near thing once too often over the last few days as they salvaged. He was so far on edge that it would only take the smallest push to send him over into the rut of mating heat… and he knew that when it finally came, he would surrender to it thankfully. The pain of holding back was a constant companion, aching all throughout the day and night, though he tried not to reveal the extent of it in front of Terri. He ran another diagnostic to see if he could build up any additional programming shields to hold the inevitable off for a little while longer. His lips pressed together in a tight frown, his mandibles clattering in frustration.

His nanos were at their limit. There would be no stopping it now.

He was growling to himself when Terri turned around and shouted to him, waving as she pointed to something that had caught her attention. Veral looked to the direction she indicated, his eyes widening with surprise. There, in the distance, a large group of humans was moving across the open desert. Large four-legged animals pulled wooden vessels across the sand.

The animals were skinny and underfed, their bones showing through their skin, but they plodded faithfully along under the direction of humans walking beside the wagon, and the sole commander seated on the vehicle. Males walked among females without conflict, often in what appeared to be mated pairs. And there were offspring! Small ones peeked out of ports on the vessels and older ones walked with the adults, a few carried in the arms of their parents. The people were tired, dirty, and almost as malnourished as the livestock, yet they were making their way west. He was witnessing an entire migrating colony of a species that should be, by all rights, extinct. Veral immediately set his ocular implant to record.

Part of his duties as a salvager was to retrieve digital documentation that could be returned to the historians and scientists of the intergalactic collective at large. It was considered almost more valuable than the raw goods he had. This sight was one that he knew would be of interest to many. The planet devastated, the civilizations decaying and dead, and yet the species stubbornly persisted. Veral drew up beside Terri, unable to look away.

"Isn't it amazing?" Terri laughed. "Kids! I don't remember the last time I saw a child."

Veral didn't reply but leaned into the female contently. He'd been away from his own home planet for so long, and far from other salvagers who traveled ceaselessly with their families, that he'd forgotten what it was like to see offspring. Even as far away as they were, he could hear the soft, reedy laughter of little ones.

At a shout, a male at the front pulled the lead vessel to a stop, the animals snorting and tossing their heads wearily as they drew to a halt. Immediately, males and females hurried to it and the others, stripping off supplies. They worked like a swarm of industrious insects bent on a task and Veral watched with interest as the rough outlines of a camp began to pop up over the hard, packed ground.

One of the males studying the landscape suddenly froze, his arm going up as he shouted, gesturing wildly. Confused, Veral turned his head and froze. His female had climbed on top of the rocks for a better look and was now completely visible to the humans below. It had not gone without notice and several males were approaching her. Terri cursed and jumped down, but it was too late. The males advanced, their faces set in stubborn lines. Veral snarled, his vibrissae expanding as he nudged Terri aside and placed his body between her and the humans. His arms fell back, circling around her as he pinned her to his back. The vibrissae rattled threateningly, and the pace of the males slowed.

"Do you hear that? I think we're getting close to a rattler's nest," one of the males observed in a hushed voice.

"All the more important that we get her, Kevin," another protested. "Women aren't safe out here alone. There's no telling how long she's been out here. She's probably half-feral. If we take her in, she'll be safe, and we'll all benefit when she chooses a man among us when she's ready. If there are rattlers nearby, then clearly she's in need of rescuing."

"I suppose," the other male agreed unenthusiastically. "Women can be a touch foolish like that... Running straight into a rattler's nest seems about right."

Veral sneered and backed up at Terri's urging. He wanted to remove their tongues for speaking in such a fashion about *his* female.

"Come on," she hissed. "Let's get going. We'll be long gone before they are even over the rise."

"I do not care for the way they are speaking of you," he snarled.

Terri laughed, though it sounded strained. "They're just being stupid. They'll give up the moment they get to the top without anything to show for it."

"They seek to damage your honor," he returned vehemently.

She shook her head. "My honor is fine. Trust me, I don't need any more trophies."

He scowled at her, taken in by the unyielding look on her face despite his disappointment. "I would gladly lay their tongues at your feet."

"Now that's a charming picture I could live without," she replied, her tug on him becoming more insistent as the clattering sound of loose rock echoed around them. "Come on, Veral. The last thing I want is them getting a good look at you and going into a panic. You don't exactly inspire peace and goodwill."

Veral cast her a curious glance. "Why would I wish to do so? It is good that they fear me upon sight. Then they will know to stay far away from me and mine."

"Of course that would be your logic," she muttered in exasperation, but he did not miss the way the corners of her lips tugged up fondly. "Come on then, my terrifying male, I do not want to be delayed with an unnecessary confrontation. Let's get our carts back to the ship so that we may rest. Besides, I want to see it. Also, you promised me that I would be able to get clean," she reminded him with a grin.

Veral groaned at the image her reminder conjured. He pictured his female in the cleansing unit taking advantage of the mineral tub. He would fill it with water and tend to her bathing before taking great pleasure in rubbing exotic, expensive oils from far-flung planets into her skin. The oils were his one pleasure, and he looked forward to sharing it with his mate. The uncomfortable pressure of his swollen civix—which had never truly reduced since its first inflammation and wouldn't until it was satisfied—pushed aggressively forward against the seam of his pouch. He panted and growled as his civix writhed, desperately seeking the feminine heat of his mate.

Unintentionally, one of his vibrissae lifted and slipped through the filaments on her head—her hair as she called it. He groaned at the simple contact; his hips thrust forward into the air in front of him helplessly. The texture was gritty from sweat, dirt, and sand. He did not find it objectionable as his vibrissae twined around her locks of hair, tugging gently. The rich scent of Terri's arousal swamped his senses, sending his systems into a frenzy.

In that state, Veral's aggression spiked as he scented the human males, and his processor tracked their movement up the hillside. A vicious growl erupted from him, his vibrissae's rattle becoming more pronounced in volume as they lifted further into the air around his head. It was the territorial sound of a male warning off a potential rival. Krono echoed the sound as he positioned himself at Terri's side, his long fangs bared.

A horrible thought occurred to Veral as the salty, pungent scent of the males drew closer. What if Terri desired to join with them? They were her own species and weren't members of the gang that had been threatening her. She may desire a human mate.

His head whipped around to look at her. "You will not mate with any of those males," he demanded.

Terri's brows climbed on her flat, expressive face. "You are honestly worried about that?"

He snarled and turned his head away, his vibrissae jerking periodically with his barely controlled aggression. "They are weak, inferior… They stink," he added with a wrinkle of his nose. He enjoyed the way his anastha smelled, but no other humans.

He was still debating what terrible things he could do to remove his rivals or discourage their pursuit when he felt a small hand slide up into his vibrissae. Small fingers wrapped around several of them before yanking firmly as a female Argurma would in mating to demand the seed of her mate. The sensation shot down to his civix, making it jerk and thump at the barrier of his pouch. A ripple of pleasure shot through his groin as he felt the seam separate more. Clicking his mandibles, he growled and turned his hot gaze onto his mate. The humans were getting louder, but their noise faded into the background as he dismissed their presence in favor of the desire surging through him for his female.

"I see I've got your attention now," she whispered, her lips quirking with amusement.

He hissed in agreement as he turned to nudge her toward his ship with his massive body. His instinctive needs were taking over, overwhelming his processors with their demands. He felt nothing but the impulse pushing through his coding to make haste and get his female into his abode. His starship was the only home he possessed, and at that moment he desired her caged within it more than anything.

Terri's smile widened at his show of dominance, her pleasure tinting the musk of her arousal. Lightly tugging again on his vibrissae, she backed in the direction that he desired her to go. Veral trilled low in his throat, his body crowding hers, his mandibles scraping through her hair, gathering her scent and taste into his receptors. With a low, rattling groan, he broke away from her.

"Enough, female. At your insistence, I will forget these males, but we must go now."

His previous goal of waiting to secure his mating until their task was complete was forgotten. He would not be able to wait for the optimal moment, but he refused to seed his female for the first time on the desert floor. He would tie his mate to him within the dwelling that would become hers by right of Argurma law.

Everything that was his would become his mate's property, and the idea thrilled him on a fundamental, primitive level. In one act, everything that he was, down to everything that she would soon own, would be imbued with his scent and nano signature. She would own it by law, but in turn he would conquer her and irrevocably tie her to him.

Surging forward over the terrain, he came close to dragging Terri behind him until, with a snarl of impatience, he flung his mate over his shoulder so that her body was wedged between his neck and the primary horn on his shoulder. Her breath left her body in a whoosh of air, but she regained it quickly enough that he was not concerned.

Terri's small hands tugged on his armor and he felt her weight shift as she did her best to lift her upper body despite the way she swayed with his every step. Her throaty laughter sent sparks of pleasure shooting over him. They gathered and shot straight down to his groin when her small hands caressed his buttocks as if studying them. He felt a sting as the flat of her hand connected with one. His hips jerked once again, his civix convulsing.

Oh, the pleasure it provided… and gave him ideas of how he might turn such a stirring touch on her own delicate backside.

"You know, you really do have a great ass," she said. "I've admired it before but obviously never this up close and personal. It is truly impressive. Especially when you're wearing nothing but a tiny scrap of cloth."

"You speak of my sadt," he grumbled as she continued to caress the muscles enticingly.

"Sadt... It's misnamed if you ask me. Looking at it definitely doesn't make me *sad*. Just very happy," she quipped. He chuffed at the wordplay as he turned and dropped his head, his nose brushing the apex of her thighs. He inhaled her scent as his own hand rose to knead the curve of her ass, eliciting a throaty moan from his mate.

Veral quickened his step, feeling the pressure of the impending breach of his pouch. Relief surged through his systems when he finally detected the energy signature of his cloaked ship. Sending himself into the mainframe of his vessel, he deactivated the cloak and opened the cargo hold. The black portal rippled and slid open at his approach. He didn't waste a precious second striding up into his ship, despite being fully aware of his mate craning her head trying to see everything at once.

"Veral, hang on... Veral!" He growled when she delivered a pinch to his asscheek. "Slow down, I want to see this. Better yet... put me down."

"You will have plenty of time to investigate at your leisure, but not now," he replied taciturnly.

He stopped at the portal leading into the main ship and paused long enough to be certain that all the collector carts were in the cargo hold and the ship's cloak was reactivated. Normally, he would attend to the carts right away, but he barely had the presence of mind to close the cargo entrance before plunging into the depths of the ship with Terri in his embrace. His blood heated as the familiar scents of his ship mixed and merged with those of his female. The end product was so perfect that every breath he drew was filled with a sense of rightness. He was only just barely aware of Krono trotting ahead of them.

Veral bypassed the cockpit and headed directly for his chambers. His seam was splitting more and more with each step and his vision clouded over with a frenzy of desire. His pulse beat out a rhythm of need that could not be denied.

He no longer wished to deny or restrain it. Caught in its fury, he couldn't recall or imagine why he attempted to do so in the first place. He burned for her and her arousal deepened in response, feeding off his own pheromones that he was now steadily releasing into the air in the confines of his territory.

"Oh, fuck," she whispered, her nose and cheek brushing against his back. "You smell so good. I can hardly describe it. Like exotic, unknown spices and the wood that I sometimes find in the closets where rich people used to live." She took another deep breath. "Amazing. I can't believe how hot it is making me. I feel like I am about ready to combust."

Although the turn of phrase sounded alarming, Veral understood the raw need behind the words. He felt it as well. His body began to prime itself, his civix pushing against his pouch. His world focused on his intense need to breed.

"Anastha," he bit out, needing to warn her. "I cannot restrain myself. It will be rough and perhaps more violent than you are used to. Do not resist. If you struggle, I will instinctively pin you in place when I am in the grips of the heat. It will not be pleasant."

"I expect you to explain all of this to me when we are both in our right minds," she said. "But trust me, babe, I have no intention of resisting. I don't think I've ever wanted to fuck this bad my entire life!"

A surprised chuff of laughter burst from him as he strode into his room—*their* room. Reverently, he stretched his mate over the bed, his body pressing briefly against hers before he pulled away to divest himself of his armor as soon as possible. The moment his groin plate came off, his civix burst through the barrier of his pouch with a sharp sensation that sent such an intense wave of pleasure through him that he wanted to drown in it, relishing every moment as his inky sex twisted in the air in front of him for the first time. Its flexible, hooked head snapped through the air as the shaft coiled. Two large tubes at either side of the head leaked fluid, lubricating his priming civix. He stared at it in fascination and alarm. It seemed larger and thicker than what he was expecting. He glanced at his mate, hoping that she wasn't alarmed by its appearance.

Instead of being afraid, Terri stared at it curiously through lust-hazed eyes, her lips parting in an intense expression of need. With a snap of his hands, he removed her clothing before prowling back up the length of her body, his massive frame wedging between her thighs. His mate shifted, a wariness beneath the haze of desire.

"Veral," she whispered. "Careful…"

Need twisted through his gut. He couldn't make sense of her warning, but nor could he find the words to inquire as to her meaning. His cock snapped restlessly, its upward movement pulling at his sack hidden within his pouch for the time being. Every yank of his civix against his root made his body shudder. He couldn't hold back. His hips slammed forward, his civix twisting and burrowing into the deep, dark heat of her sex as he plowed in one long thrust until their hips met.

14

*T*erri gasped. She was wet enough that she didn't feel more than a pinch as her untried sex stretched, yielding as his massive sex rooted deep within her. She felt it twisting and rubbing against her inner walls as it plunged deeper, the strange, almost hook-shaped head searching for something as it ground against the delicate cluster of nerves. It struck the sensitive spot with enough force that it had her arching up and wailing as her belly clenched with an orgasm that whipped through her with the force of the violent sandstorms that regularly swept over the city.

Through all of it, she was anchored by his arms and the weight of his pelvis against hers. Even his vibrissae threaded through her hair, twining and stroking as he crooned to her. She clung to him, though his cock was so unlike anything she'd ever imagined. It moved on its own as Veral began to pump his hips, grinding down at the end of each thrust with a rolling, almost purring sound from his vibrating mandibles. Terri reached out and grasped the horns protruding from his shoulders. They were short but curved upward, providing perfect handholds to give her stability and control in the storm that swept over her.

Although frightened a little by its intensity, she surrendered to it, lightning licking over her flesh every time their pelvises crashed together. Even caught up in her ecstasy, and inexperienced as she was, she knew that this was not just sex.

Did sex feel like one was being claimed down to the deepest, hidden recesses of her being?

She didn't have the mental space to even think of it clearly. Veral demanded everything from her as he rocked into her, his cock twisting within her every time he retreated as if protesting and attempting to worm its way again close to her womb, but then stiffening eagerly as he thrust deep again. It bumped, the hooked tip making her sex clench at its every contact against the mouth of her womb.

Terri arched her back, lifting her hips eagerly. She could feel something building and she raced toward it, needed it with a desperation that was unfamiliar. She *needed* relief, for the dam to break, yet it seemed elusive, making her whimper. Though his size made it difficult for her to wrap her legs around him, she hooked her calves, pressing the heel of her feet against him in silent demand.

Veral seemed to understand. He growled, the sound layering with the purring of his mandibles, and his pace increased.

She wiggled against his seeking cock. She'd released her legs to dig her heels into his bed and push herself up against him. His arms wrapped around her hips, drawing her higher as he sat up, driving down into her at such an angle that it set her nerves on fire. It felt... different. Whatever it was, it was intensifying every sensation as he rutted into her.

When the explosive orgasm came, it caught her off-guard, snapping through her so powerfully that she couldn't even summon the voice to scream out her pleasure. Her mouth gaped wide, an airy shriek breaking loose as something lodged deep within her. Veral's purring ceased and he voiced a shaky growl, his mandibles flaring wide. He crushed his lips against the base of her throat as his cock began to jerk within her, whipping strangely unlike its previous movement as it attached to her womb. Hot ejaculations sprayed into her, covering the walls of her cunt, but the movement and pressure set off another orgasm. Her belly contracted and spasmed as it accepted the gift that Veral provided. That time, she did scream.

He let out a final roar as his mandibles descended, the hooked edge of each piercing into the side of her neck as a hot fluid seeped out of them directly into her bloodstream. The pain startled her before a new pleasure welled up within her that had her wailing with ecstasy.

She was coming down from bliss when she felt his mandibles release her. His twin tongues slipped over her throat, seeping something sticky on the wounds. She watched in fascination as he lifted his head. She saw tiny tube-like tips at the end of his tongues before they closed, and his tongues retreated back into his mouth. Gasping from the raw sensations flooding her body, she attempted to move her hips. She didn't get far. Veral pressed his pelvis firmly against hers, holding her in place.

"Veral? What's going on?" she said, her wiggling attempts renewing until she moved just enough to feel a sharp pain.

"Do not!" he growled, a low painful hiss mirroring her own gasp. She shuddered around his invading length, rhythmically, sending small tremors shooting through her. "We are locked as my body completes implantation. If you move before my civix releases your womb, it will cause us both pain."

"*Implantation?*" she squeaked in alarm. Instinctively, she kicked against him in hope of dislodging him. He growled and held her tighter in response.

"The first mating culminates in implantation to secure the bonds between the male and female. Sometimes a fetus thrives, but often not in the first attempt with the body chemistry still altering and aligning," he muttered into her skin.

Her eyes widened. "*Fetus!* As in baby?"

Veral gave her a puzzled look. "Do you not know how offspring are conceived?"

She flushed. "I do, but I didn't think it would be possible between different species."

He jerked his head in a nod. "It is untried to my knowledge. It is possible that we will never spawn offspring, but that will not stop my body from trying to seed yours."

She cleared her throat and swallowed as she shifted against him. "So, when you say seed, you're literally depositing into me."

He cocked his head, studying her reaction.

"Yes, I release both the seed and semen. When it latches onto your womb and draws nutrients into its body, its genetic code will adjust to include your own chromosomes."

Terri panted. "I have no idea what you're talking about, but I assume you mean it'll include something of myself in it if it survives."

"Yes," he responded.

She lifted one hand to her neck. "You bit me too," she observed tonelessly, a bit shell-shocked over the whole baby implantation thing.

"Both my semen and the toxins from my mandibles carry the necessary nanos into your blood to secure our bond, along with my chemical imprint. It is both instinctive to my species and an advantage of our cybernetic pair bondings. My tongue ventors release a hormonal sap necessary to seal the wound afterward. That is the cap you feel," he explained as his eyes narrowed on her hand.

"Will it change me?" she whispered nervously, her fingers still twitching around the dry caps over her wound.

"Minimally. Your aging will slow to be in time with mine, the nanos repairing your cells and any damage you sustain. You will heal faster and will survive even critical wounds with proper care. That is all you will experience without the interference of the Council."

Terri's fingers on one hand dug into his forearm where it had slipped upon releasing the horn protruding from his shoulder. "What would the Council do?"

"Nothing." He growled fiercely. "I will prevent it. You are *mine*!"

"Yours," she murmured in agreement. "And you're mine, right?"

His icy eyes gleamed down at her as he dropped his nose to nuzzle her jaw. "Eternally."

Her eyes slid shut in relief. Eventually his body shifted off hers, though their sexes were still locked together, and he eased them onto their sides to rest comfortably upon the luxurious bedding. She hadn't noticed it until then, but she snuggled her cheek against the slick softness and sighed appreciatively.

Veral lay there and held her for some time before his sex finally dislodged, warm cum spilling out over her thighs. He did not leave except to search out a cleansing cloth to wipe their mingled fluids off them. Once that was accomplished, he rejoined her, wrapping his body more comfortably around hers. His body warmed hers as his mandibles renewed their purring vibration, lulling her to sleep.

15

The mineral tub wasn't what Terri expected. She watched it rise out of the floor in the center of the stark cleansing unit. Just moments before, there had been nothing but four walls, each armed with a nozzle, with a larger one overhead. The tub lifted directly below the overhead nozzle. The moment the rectangular bath clicked into place, Veral touched a panel on the wall. To her surprise, a stream of shimmery powder poured out of the nozzle into the tub below. It ran for several minutes before shutting off.

She looked at the few inches of powder and frowned. Was that it?

Veral drew her back away from the tub and tapped another panel. Water spouted down from above. The contact with the powder made it fizz and pop before swirling and mixing with the water. It appeared almost translucent and pearly in the comfortable lighting of the cleansing unit. It was pretty, but she was uncertain about bathing in it.

"Is that going to be safe for me? Human bodies are pretty sensitive."

"Of course. I have taken thorough scans of you and have

uploaded the information to my ship. This mixture of mineral bath is designed for optimal health benefits for both of us."

She turned and smiled up at him flirtatiously. "Both of us, huh? Were you planning on joining me, O dark and deadly?"

"I am," he said with a smirk. He wore nothing but the simple band of cloth he called a sadt, but he unfastened it and allowed it to drop to the floor. For the first time, Terri was treated to the sight of her mate naked in full light. Her mouth went dry at the corded muscles of his arms and torso. His longer body had more abdominal muscles than she'd ever seen on a human, each one carved out perfectly in nine pairs trailing down to his navel. He didn't have a belly button, just a slight indentation between muscles that she was curious to explore with her tongue.

His sex, however, was almost completely hidden. All that was visible was a thick pouch of pale gray flesh, a stark contrast against his black scales. As she looked at it curiously, there was movement within moments before the black hooked tip of his phallus pushed through. Only the head was visible, and it stayed there for a short time before slowly slipping back into his pouch.

"Whoa," she whispered and dragged her eyes away from his pouch to his muscular legs. His feet were almost like a human's except the toes were longer and more curved. She suspected that, like his hands, each digit contained a retractable claw that could be lethal.

Veral trilled, catching her attention. "Do you enjoy what you see?" he asked, throwing her words back at her.

Terri grinned shamelessly up at him. "Without a doubt."

He trilled again in obvious pleasure, his mandibles vibrating in a purr as he scooted closer to her. Large hands reaching out to her, he stripped every piece of clothing from her body. Once she was completely bare, he closed his hands around her waist and lifted her effortlessly into the tub. Terri gasped at the touch of the pleasantly warm water. After years of bathing in cold water, lacking the luxury of a stable home where water was heated since her mother died, she'd forgotten how good hot water felt. Her gasp turned into a moan as she sank into the shimmering water.

Veral's mandibles clicked together. "Your sounds of enjoyment are a delight, anastha."

He stepped into the large tub, settling comfortably with a hiss. Reaching forward, he pulled her over to him so that she was cradled against his chest, the water sloshing at the edges of the tub though never quite spilling over.

Terri relaxed into the heat of his body, all too aware of the way his cock jerked in its pouch before sliding out like a firebrand against her ass. It twisted against her, trying to tunnel toward her sex. Veral groaned and his arms wrapped around her, holding her tight. She wiggled against him, her desire sparking at the feel of his cock caressing her ass. Her mate growled and yanked her up so that her bottom no longer rested on the smooth material of the tub. His cock wedged itself beneath her as it burrowed persistently into her channel, every writhing motion of his phallus grinding against her clit, sending pleasure shooting through her.

He didn't move. He held her in place and gathered a small padded cloth that when rubbed emitted a pleasant-smelling cleanser. He washed her leisurely, soaping her breasts and belly as his cock twisted and writhed within her. Veral interrupted his washing to gently pinch one of her nipples as the head of his sex bumped a delicious spot within her.

All too soon, his hand moved away, and he continued to explore her body with soapy hands as his cock stroked her insides. She moaned and tried to shift to give herself some relief, but he held her fast, pinned to his pelvis. Soon his moans and growls joined hers and Terri's body began to quiver, wound tight. His swollen cock dove and flexed once more, brushing a sensitive spot deep within her and she clenched around him, her hips jerking as her orgasm swept over, soon followed by Veral's.

Her mate growled and panted behind her, his body shaking slightly as he gently pulled her off his phallus, allowing it to retreat back within his pouch. His touch felt gentle as he washed between her legs before tending to himself as they lay together, soaking within the hot water.

At long last, he gathered her in his arms and stepped out of the tub. Touching the same panel that brought it up, the tub drained and sank back into the floor. Another panel started a stream of water sluicing down over them from the nozzle above, and the side nozzles sprayed them from all sides.

"Close your eyes," he said.

She obliged and discovered that a sweet-smelling substance was spraying on her body and over her head. Lifting her arms, she massaged her scalp to remove any lingering dirt and grime. Within minutes, it shifted back to water, rinsing them thoroughly.

The water shut off and she wiped her fingers over her eyes to remove some of the excess water. She let out a startled squeak of surprise when hot air blew from vents in the walls, drying her rapidly. When they shut off, Terri stood still a moment longer to make sure no other surprises would be sprung on her. Laughing, Terri stepped out of the cleansing unit. Veral chuffed in amusement as he followed her out.

Slipping a long silky robe of the most vivid shade of blue around her, he led her through the ship, letting her explore to her leisure as he pointed out the features of his spacecraft and what specific things did. She was particularly fascinated with the food replicator. The clothing generator soon became her second favorite when he provided a smaller black armored suit to fit over her frame.

"Only for when we are out there. I much prefer seeing the robes on you. They highlight your beauty. The armor, however, will keep you safer to my liking," he said as he sealed the clasps into place. With those words, he brushed his nose and mandibles over the top of her head before leading her toward the cargo bay. "Come, anastha. I have work to complete here before we can return to Phoenix."

Terri allowed herself to be pulled along with him, though she was almost disappointed that she had to return to the city so soon. When she was in the ship with Veral, she could almost forget her pitiful life of scavenging for scraps.

Soon, though, that would be behind her. It was a comforting thought.

16

"Just how long do Argurma pregnancies last?" Terri asked.

Veral glanced up at her from the side of the collector cart that he was sealing and putting into locked mode. She was looking down at her belly, her brow knitted together in concentration while one hand played gently among Krono's vibrissae. The dorashnal leaned against her, his scales nearly quivering in an expression of bliss. Veral's own vibrissae moved as his processors lit up with images of his mate swollen with his offspring. He was intrigued by the idea as he latched the cart in place in the hold. Though it was premature to expect to be greeted with young on their first joining, he couldn't deny that he lusted for it.

"We evolved in a manner that provides slow development to reduce physical stress on the females in a desert environment. This means that the fetus remains very small, building its complex systems over a two-year period. Within the first three lunar cycles of the third year is when it matures rapidly to prepare for birth. The two years are utilized to collect plenty of food and water for these final three months when the female remains in her domicile attended by her mate."

Terri's jaw dropped in what he now knew meant surprise. It

was a curious lack of muscular control in the face for the species when they were scared or startled. It was most entertaining in his mate, though he suspected that he would get enjoyment out of it from any of those that he killed as well, although in a different sense. When done by his mate, he found it oddly endearing.

"Pregnant for *three years!*"

Ah, it seemed that horror was also involved. How fascinating. His mandibles automatically began to vibrate to soothe his mate. She blinked at the sound, but her body quickly began to relax, not unlike that of the females of his own species.

"Just so you know, in humans we carry the egg… uh, seed, I guess you say, which the male fertilizes. But human babies only gestate for roughly nine months."

"Your species must have once reproduced very quickly like prey animals," he observed. "On Argurumal, only small creatures and prey animals reproduce yearly, usually during our brief wet season."

"So you're comparing me to livestock…" she said slowly.

Not wishing to displease his mate, he searched his memory banks and amended his statement. "The great enthar is a massive, intelligent creature that swims across the oceans of moving sand of Argurumal. They deliver one pup a year," he added thoughtfully.

Her brows shot upward. "Did you just compare me to a desert whale?"

"They are dangerous predators, with long necks that allow them to pick off warriors at their leisure," he offered placatingly.

"Make that the Loch Ness Monster of the sands." He frowned. Perhaps he said something that upset his female. Such concerns were allayed when she burst out laughing. "I fucking love it!"

He gave a low click of his mandibles as he returned his attention to his task. Once all the carts were secured, he went to the wall storage unit and retrieved more collector cart discs. Snapping them into place on his belt, he gestured for Terri to join him. She immediately took her place beside him. Nudging Terri out of the cargo hold into the hot desert air and allowing room from Krono to squeeze through, Veral sealed his ship once more.

His mate grinned up at him and leaned in, wrapping her arms around his torso to bestow her affection upon him. It was not the way of Argurma to touch when not engaged in coitus, but he found that he enjoyed it. Her embrace was welcome, and he trilled low in his throat in response. He could feel his civix trying to work out of his pouch once more, eager for the tight, hot sheath of his mate, but he drew away, allowing only a moment between them for his mandibles to slide affectionately over the top of her head and his vibrissae to stroke over and through her hair.

They traversed the sands side-by-side. Although his gait naturally outstripped hers, he reined in his steps to keep pace with her. Only Krono struck out ahead, his forked tails waving behind him. Although in their days together previously he had been comfortable allowing her to trail behind him, now his systems demanded that he keep her firmly within his sight despite everything around them being calm and undisturbed.

"Do you think that the migrants are still camped out on the desert?" Terri asked.

Veral snapped his vibrissae, unconcerned. "If they are wise, they will not linger where the Reapers might easily ambush them. They should be far from here by now."

"What does that say about us then?" she returned with a slow smile.

He chuffed, his vibrissae tangling in her hair and gently tugging on the locks playfully. "It says that your male is far more dangerous than any of them and, if they were wise, the Reapers would flee instead."

Terri's grin widened before it faltered. "You wouldn't have really hurt the migrants, would you?"

Veral clicked his mandibles thoughtfully. "If they attempted to take you from me or harm you in any way, I would. I have little concern for those not tied to me."

His mate frowned in disapproval. He admired her soft heart

even if it was inconvenient. "That's not very compassionate," she countered.

He chuffed in amusement at her observation. "Argurma live by codes of action and obligation. I might concede to serve my people because it is within the framework of my purpose to serve them, but my bonds and sympathies do not extend far beyond you and any offspring we might have." He paused, considering his progenitor. "I would not be as my sire was. I believe that I would care very much for our young."

A happy look returned to his mate's face, and he continued by her side contentedly until the roar of engines in the distance ripped him away from his peace. His arm snapped out, stilling his mate as his mandibles extended and his mouth opened, drawing in the scents of the desert surrounding them. Whatever was occurring was far enough away that he didn't sense any disruption in their immediate vicinity. But the sound of the engines was unmistakably that of the Reapers verging into the desert. As they came over the rise, he was able to see the metallic glint in the distance.

Scanning the red and yellow desert, it didn't take him long to locate the caravan. The camp was still erected, males and females moving about as their offspring milled around and chased after each other in their play. A rattling growl rose in his throat in accompaniment to his vibrating vibrissae. They were storing their belongings back in their vessels but were going about it leisurely beneath the brutal heat of the sun bearing down on them.

"Oh, fuck," Terri whispered at his side, her eyes turning attentively to the direction of his focus. "They didn't leave!"

"Foolish to risk offspring in such a way."

They hadn't seen the Reapers, but he knew the exact moment when they did. A cry went through the people as adults picked the younglings up from the ground and ran toward their vessels.

He turned away with disinterest and no little contempt. He felt no discomfort over surrendering them to their fate. He came to a stop, however, when he felt his mate grip his arm tightly. He chirped at her inquiringly, his gaze going down to her hand clenched on his armored wrist just above the horn curving out at the joint.

Her eyes were imploring as she looked up at him. "Veral, we can't leave them to the Reapers. *Please*! We have to help them."

He regarded her steadily and cocked his head. "I would not risk my mate for the wellbeing of strangers too foolish to safeguard themselves from enemies."

She took a breath and met his gaze directly. "I'm not asking you to. I'm asking you to do this for me. Be compassionate and merciful on my behalf. Help them like I would if I had the ability. I will stay out of the way and remain safe, I promise... Just help them, damn you! If you don't, I will."

Veral turned to face her fully, anger radiating through him as his vibrissae lifted into the air, thrashing around him. "You will not disobey me!"

"Then do what I ask!" she snapped.

"Very well," he bit out, his vibrissae flaring out around him as he focused his attention on the encampment below.

Without another word, he lifted Terri into his arms and raced toward the caravan, utilizing all his enhanced speed. Although he raced down from the slopes, he knew the Reapers barreling toward the encampment would make contact first. He would not arrive in time to prevent the slaughter. He growled viciously as Terri shouted when the first of the Reapers struck, bringing down a mature, unarmed male. The male valiantly attempted to fight him off, swinging his crude weapon through the air.

The Reaper toyed with him, laughing and taunting, delivering wound after wound with each retort until the injured male succumbed. The female at his side shrieked, rushing back to her mate with a club upraised. Even from his greater distance, his optical enhancements saw that her eyes were wild with grief even as he caught and zeroed in on the faint sounds of her sobs amid the chaos. The male circled her, trying to snatch up the female. Every time he came near, she struck him. It wasn't enough to do any true damage but gave her a small reprieve before he was on her again.

The final time she swung her club, he caught it and ripped it out of her hands. With a shout, he struck her with it. The crack from the delivered force was loud and the female fell to the dirt a short distance from her mate she'd attempted to defend.

The Reaper did not last long himself, however. Krono, outstripping Veral in speed, lunged upon the male, dragging him down. His terrible teeth quickly ended the pitiful human's life. Chest heaving as he panted, gore splashed over him, Krono made a terrible sight, but no one seemed to notice him. They were too focused on the males spilling into the encampment.

All around males and females shouted in panic as the Reapers flooded in, some on small two-wheeled vehicles, riding alone or in pairs. Others were packed together on what Terri called pickups with males, jumping from the back amid the prey, snatching up females and bludgeoning men to spare the ammunition. The migrants ducked behind their wagon, seeking safety in numbers as they pulled knives and whatever else they could find to protect their offspring. Any female who resisted too much was killed in the attempt to restrain them. More were killed in obvious bouts of bloodlust among the Reapers. In consequence, many females died before Veral arrived. His processors recorded every scream into his memory. When the first offspring wailed helplessly for its mother as she was gutted by a laughing Reaper, it triggered something within his mind.

In that moment, Veral understood hate. Every offspring's cry served to work him into a fury so that when he dropped among them, he was truly the likeness of death.

Setting Terri beside the wagon, he spun around and flung himself at the nearest Reaper, his long, secondary fangs sliding down over his primary teeth, and his retractable claws lengthening for battle. He did not have his blaster, but he did not need it. His processors targeted each male and he leaped upon them, shredding them with claws and fang in the old way. His brethren would find such a method of killing uncivilized and brutish, but such concerns didn't touch him other than a distant acknowledgment. The old

ways served him well, even better with his systems online calculating the most expedient way to destroy his target.

Blood flowed like a crimson river around him and he rejoiced in
it, triumphant in battle as he conquered his foes. He was almost
amused by the way the desert greedily sucked the liquid of the
spilled blood into the parched ground with each human he tore
apart. Yet, no matter in the intensity of his warrior's bloodlust, he
always kept Terri in his peripheral vision. His processors studied
her as she crouched over the children huddled around her. The few
remaining females, heavily wounded, scrambled to her side, their
arms clutching their offspring.

He would allow nothing to get through him.

It was, in truth, a relatively small number of Reapers who had
been sent after the caravan, yet only a pitiful handful of them had
gotten away, dragging females with them. Veral snarled in frustration that even one evaded him. He snatched one off the back of a
truck as it peeled away, the male's body colliding with the ground
before he opened the human's belly. Still, it wasn't enough. Those
few Reapers who escaped did so with their shrieking victims flung
over the back of their two-wheel vehicles or piled into the trucks.

Veral walked among the remains of the Reapers, his vibrissae
waving around him, rattling their menacing song, and he surveyed
the destruction he'd carried out on his mate's behalf. He felt
nothing but elation as he stared at the ruins of males he had
destroyed by his own hand. Their deaths had given the females
time to escape to safety. He felt satisfied by the great nest of
corpses that surrounded him, their limbs tangled together wherever
they overlapped. He could feel the wide, terrible grin of predatory
triumph stretch over his face as he looked over the carnage.

It was the soft, shuddering cry of females that finally drew his
attention. Spinning around, he stalked over to them, Krono loping
to his side. His gaze fastened on none but his own female, watching
him with a curious light in her eye. His lips quirked in amusement
though it soon turned to a disdainful sneer as every female whose
life he'd saved and offspring he'd preserved retreated, holding their

younglings clenched to their chests. Not one of them remained near Terri as he approached, and he felt his contempt rise. They had no way of knowing if he was a threat to his mate and yet they abandoned her despite the fact that she'd done everything in her power to protect them.

He growled intolerantly at a female who recoiled from him, weeping uncontrollably. Terri frowned at the aggressive noise and attempted to soothe and reassure them. They didn't respond other than to weep amongst themselves. One female, an older one among them with a pair of older offspring following close to her, eyed him warily as she conversed with Terri in low tones. Separated only by a short distance, he could have heard their conversation had he wished, but instead he waited for his mate to return to his side.

At length, Terri joined him again, a concerned look on her expressive face. Even covered in gore, she did not flinch from him like the other females did. Instead, she stood beside him fearlessly, her head tilted back to meet his eye.

He flung an arm open, gesturing to the cowering females in disbelief. "These are who you wish to preserve? You would stand between them and their enemy and yet all they can do is cower and weep when there is any possibility of you being injured."

"They're scared, Veral," Terri argued. "I don't expect them to stand between us. They don't know you like I do. It is natural for them to be afraid. They were on their way to the coast, where they heard that a large sanctuary city was recently established. The Reapers aren't an anomaly. Similar gangs have been striking all through the interior, but they hadn't expected to encounter one out here. They lost half of their women and a quarter of their children to this raid."

"They were careless and suffered for it," he snapped.

Several females whimpered and shied away, while others shot him angry looks.

Good. Let them hate him and learn to be strong for their offspring.

He glowered at them in turn. "This is no universe for the weak.

Learn this lesson well, for others shall follow behind me now that this world has been recorded and logged. That you dislike it doesn't matter. Hate me if it makes you feel better but be stronger than you are. Your offspring are dependent on you. Will you curl onto the ground and allow yourself and your young to die because you are too frightened to continue by yourself?" he sneered. "Mate and forge strong alliances but remain strong, steady, and observant. Take nothing for granted." He growled in parting before allowing his mate to pull him away.

Her brows lifted at him. "A little harsh, weren't you?"

"I spoke nothing but the truth. Anything less would be dishonorable and teach them nothing of how to survive."

"Maybe," she agreed slowly. "But humans usually couch unpleasant truths in ways that are not quite as offensive to the one receiving them. It's part of being compassionate."

"Then I shall leave compassion to you. I am concerned more with the survival of their offspring. I do not hold with any adult who would allow their grief to damage their young."

"Ah, you're talking about your father then?" she said softly.

"I am speaking of him and them. Their offspring deserve better."

Terri nodded slowly. She opened her mouth, the tip of her tongue touching her lip thoughtfully as she visibly searched for the words she wished to say. He waited patiently, his attention completely on her.

"Veral, we need to talk."

"We are speaking," he grumbled.

"No. I mean I'm going to have to alter our agreement," she said with a tiny smile.

He scrutinized her silently, not moving, as he attempted to process her meaning. She shifted from one foot to the other, though she met his eyes with a steely resolve.

"Speak plainly of your intentions, female."

"I can't help you salvage right now. They need my help."

He blinked at her in surprise. "You speak of the coast. They require your aid to get there?" He shook his head at the glaring fault in her plans. "By your own admission, you have never left this settlement. You would be a disastrous guide."

"True." She laughed dryly, her smile slipping. "No, that's not what they need from me. I'm going into the Reapers' camp. Before you say anything, no, they didn't ask me to do it. I volunteered. The women and children they stole—I couldn't live with myself if I didn't at least try to save them."

His eyes shifted to the cluster of females and offspring behind her. They watched him warily as if expecting him to lash out and attack his female.

Moving in closer, he dropped his head close to her cheek where he could breathe in her natural perfume as he spoke in a low whisper, his breath fanning her face. "It is dangerous. Do you forget that you are mine?"

"Impossible to forget," she whispered. "I swear I'm not leaving you or abandoning you in any fashion. I'm not your father. I won't forget you just because something else demands my attention. I will take care to remain safe and once it's done, I'm all yours once more."

Veral growled with impatience, his vibrissae lifting in a show of dominance. In response, all the females stammered, their bodies pressing in close around Terri, though his mate looked on, entirely unimpressed by his display. He snorted, amused by his mate and insulted down to his circuitry by the other females.

He wouldn't harm his mate or allow harm to come to her.

She was his—his *everything*. She was the safest female on the entire planet.

He wanted to object. However, his female was insisting on aiding them, and they were clinging to her like sap beetles of Octnartova. It was doubtful that he would be able to convince his mate to abandon her plan. If he wanted to safeguard Terri, he understood, somewhat reluctantly, that it required a departure from their original agreement. He shook out his vibrissae in disgust.

Very well. He would be flexible.

He returned his focus to his female.

"We will delay our salvage and help these humans." Veral smirked to himself as her mouth dropped open but kept his expression blank and unaffected.

"Wait! You're going to help?"

"You are under contract to me *and* you are my mate. That contract has yet to be satisfied and I refuse to allow my mate to wander into danger without my protection. I will not let you go against the Reapers alone. Besides being my female, the debt remains between us."

Terri smirked up at him. "The debt... I suppose you have a point. All right, my mate, I will allow you to help me since you asked oh so graciously."

With another long look in his direction, she turned away and waved at the other females. "Come on! Let's get to shelter before the Reapers decide to investigate!"

Shuffling in a mostly sedate manner, many of them keening quietly to themselves, they left the abandoned bodies of their mates and companions. Clutching their children tightly to them, the females followed Terri and Veral away from the dusty sea of blood. Some flinched from time to time as Krono occasionally circled near, his muzzle and chest soaked with the blood of his kills, but otherwise they made steady progress into the fallen city.

erri offered some water to a small child who looked up at her with wide, scared brown eyes. Everyone was exhausted as they leaned against each other crammed into the room. It had been a long walk, especially for the children. After the dust had settled, it hadn't taken them long to notice that both of the skinny mares had been killed during the gang's attack. That had been the first sign that made her realize helping the women wasn't going to be easy.

Terri had felt her first moments of frustration when a large portion of the women refused to do anything other than wring their hands. They didn't want to go through their things and pack supplies that could be reasonably carried. They just whimpered as a handful of the women among them dug through the wagons and loaded themselves down with as much as they could carry. Veral spent a good part of their trek back to Phoenix glaring at them.

Even now, sitting in clusters around the living room along the few remaining walls, they did nothing but complain about being hungry and thirsty while Terri worked to ration out the supplies with the help of the women who were among the lead organizers for their caravan. Truth be told, she was beginning to lose her patience with their helplessness. If it weren't for the few competent women among them struggling to see to everyone's needs despite grieving for their own losses, she would likely have yielded to Veral's insistence to let them fend for themselves.

It wasn't a charitable thought, but she was exhausted and feeling less and less inclined to be magnanimous with every passing hour that she had to tend to them. Despite the number of women who'd fought off the Reapers, and the large handful of them who were dragged away kicking and screaming, Terri had come to find out that most of the women that she was stuck with were the ones who had hidden inside the wagons. She had nothing against hiding —she'd done plenty of it in her own time—but their unwillingness to do anything was quickly eroding her patience. She barely kept herself from making unpleasant comments already. Sooner or later, she was going to crack and go full crazy woman on them.

Josie, a matronly woman of forty-five, scowled from where she stood at Terri's side. She had a ladle in the hand fisted on her hip as she finished ladling broth into bowls for the women. Although she hadn't warmed up to Veral, she at least didn't cower from him whenever he approached Terri. She was perhaps only a bit less impatient with foolishness than he was. Josie possessed a sharp eye and an even sharper tongue for those who tried her patience. She was currently glaring at a young woman who was sulking over the meager ration she'd been given while ignoring the two-year-old who cried and tugged at her breast as he tried to climb into her lap. Josie snorted in disapproval.

"Your guy is a bit rough around the edges, but he wasn't wrong about one thing," she mumbled.

Terri arched an eyebrow at the other woman. "Oh?"

Josie gestured at the small group of women. "I told my Matt several times that these girls were being coddled. The men were spoiling them, insisting on doing everything for them. It wasn't good for them. He insisted that as soon as we got to the sanctuary that the girls wouldn't need to worry about struggling to survive. Told me not to worry. Now look at them, caught in their grief, helpless as children while they ignore their babies. They aren't going to do a thing for themselves. Like the rest of us aren't grieving too. Who would feed us if we all collapsed as they are, taking the luxury of doing as if it's their right?" She made a sound of disgust in the back of her throat, one hand coming up to wipe away the tears at the mention of her newly departed husband. "If they weren't so afraid of your guy, I wouldn't doubt they would be trying to latch onto him. I would watch for that anyway, because Lacey over there has that look about her like she's about to get brave."

Terri sighed. "Of all things for her to focus on. She would be better off seeing to herself and her child. She has no chance of gaining anything from Veral other than his ire."

"Hmph, that was what my daughter Becky thought until Lacey got her hooks into her man. He started sneaking the girl extra rations whenever she complained and spent all his time with her because she said she was scared to be alone. Eventually, he fathered a child on her and decided that Lacey needed him more. She used it to her advantage, getting him to take care of her. My poor Becky took it hard, but she's a fighter. Those men don't know what they're in for keeping her against her will. I hope she kills a couple in their sleep," Josie ground out.

She gave Terri a troubled look. "Now that her man's gone, it won't be long before Lacey looks for someone else to provide for her. If she or any of these other girls get it into their minds that they will be well cared for by your guy, they'll do everything in their power to win him. This world isn't kind to those who aren't strong, as you know. They will see it as a matter of survival to find someone to protect and care for them."

"How can they even tell that Veral is male?" Terri blurted out in surprise. "I didn't even know it until he told me."

Josie chuckled, her eyes gleaming with humor and sympathy. "The way he tends to you gives it away. And sometimes the front of him bulges out a bit when he's close to you. His armor must have some impressive give to it to allow that kind of flexibility," she observed wryly.

Terri felt her cheeks heat. Well, she *had* asked. Despite the fact that she didn't like other women staring at Veral, it was at least good to know the facts of the matter.

"I'm not worried." She laughed convincingly despite the twinge of anxiety that made itself known.

Josie made a doubtful sound in her throat. "If you say so. Still, the sooner we can get to the sanctuary, the better. There will be plenty of men happy to take them off my hands."

Terri smiled, but her eyes strayed again to the young woman ignoring her toddler. The baby had finally managed to wrestle his mother's breast free and was hungrily suckling despite her apathy. Lacey's head was lowered, but from between the long tangle of her hair, Terri could see that the woman's eyes were following Veral's every movement. Lacey was afraid but there was something speculative in her eyes. Or maybe Terri was just imagining it.

She knew that Veral wouldn't be interested in the other female; he barely tolerated being near them. Still, she couldn't help feeling a bit exhausted at the idea of having to deal with another woman trying to wheedle her way into his affections. It wouldn't work, but the thought of the woman even trying made her want to throw her out into the street to fend for herself against the Reapers.

Once again, the thought wasn't that kind, but Lacey had better watch herself lest Terri be tempted too far.

Frowning, she began to instinctively search out her mate. Turning to go to him, she ran into the solid wall of a male's armored abdomen. Teetering precariously, she squeaked until her mate's arms wrapped around her, anchoring her to his front. Terri sighed and melted into him, resting her head against his chest as his vibrissae slid over her hair. Even the gentle scrape of his claws over her back helped her relax against him.

Terri lifted her head to meet his gaze, but instead of seeing him looking down at her possessively, he was scowling at Josie. No doubt he'd heard every word that the other woman said. His eyes were still tracking her angrily, not that she seemed disturbed by it, but he paused to hiss at Lacey when she attempted to sidle nearer.

The girl blanched and backed away so fast that she stumbled, nearly tripping over Krono when he darted around her, leading a train of children chasing after him. With her hand fisted over her chest, Lacey dropped back to her place on the floor beside where her little one had fallen asleep on a pile of rags. Terri snickered into his chest as his arms tightened around her. He apparently decided that the other females were no longer worthy of his attention, because his jaw dropped beside her cheek and his mandibles vibrated their comforting, humming purr.

His nose brushed the side of her face. "Do not worry about these females, anastha," he said in a low voice. "You are my mate. I belong to you as much as you belong to me. My species doesn't feel the effects of desire until we already form an emotional and mental bond with our female. It cannot be reversed or overridden by the presence of another." He inhaled slowly, drawing her scent into his lungs. "They can never compare to my mate. I will never let you go," he hissed.

Terri relaxed in his arms and smiled up at him. "I know. I just don't look forward to beating weepy, clinging women off you with a stick."

One horned brow raised. "I might enjoy watching my female demonstrate her dominance. If you wish to strike them away from me, I will not stop you," he trilled with pleasure, sending a tingle up her spine.

"I'll keep that in mind," she murmured as her fingers slid over the armor protecting his belly. Veral made an approving sound and nuzzled her before stepping out of her reach. She pouted up at him, but he responded with a chuff of laughter.

"I will see to gathering what we need to enter the human compound. Inform me if these females bother you. You have worked enough for their comfort. They can get anything else they need. Rest, anastha," he demanded, his eyes narrowing on her until she nodded. Pleased, his mandibles rattled, his hand caressing her hair briefly before he strode away.

She smiled after him, his dark form wading through the smaller

women who scattered out of his way without the least bit of provo-
cation. He ducked into the hallway leading to the rooms. The
nursery was the smallest room in the wreckage of the house, but it
was comfortable and cozy for them. They agreed to allow the other
women to make use of the other three rooms. She had a feeling that
most of the women would cram into the master bedroom. It was
already difficult separating them from each other. She would probably have to herd them into the room when night fell. She debated
just letting them stay in the remains of the living room if they
insisted, just to save her the headache, but she couldn't do that. It
wasn't safe.

At least she wasn't going to have to worry about Josie and her
friends. They would likely make themselves comfortable in one of
the other rooms and enjoy the relative privacy compared to those
who would be crowded in together. Terri was just glad that she and
Veral had a room to themselves. She didn't even bother suggesting
that they open their room up for use. Her mate wouldn't have
tolerated it. He was jealously possessive over their room, warning
away any woman who so much as touched the door.

At that moment, laughter broke out in the center of the room.
Terri looked over and grinned at the source of the disruption.
Krono lay on the floor, his mouth gaping in an alien equivalent of a
canine grin as children circled around him. Some of the smaller
ones were snuggling up against him, playing with his vibrissae,
while a little girl was busy crowning the brute of a beast with
wreaths of wildflowers that she'd plucked from around the house.
The happy squealing of children rung out as they were licked by
the dorashnal's huge tongue. A pair of mothers giggled as they
watched.

One of the women stepped over to Terri, a concerned look on
her face. She had a very upset seven-year-old by the hand.

"Is that thing safe? Mandy wants to play with it like the other
children... but I don't know. I've never seen such a creature, and
the mutated animals tend to be aggressive."

"He is perfectly fine. He isn't a mutated coyote or anything like that. Krono is a dorashnal… He's Veral's companion. An alien dog, more or less," Terri explained.

The woman went pale and swallowed. "Oh, I see."

She didn't seem all that comforted by the information.

Terri smiled reassuringly and tried again. "Dorashnals are good animals and very smart. He won't hurt them. I believe Veral once told me that he's had Krono from the time he was very young."

"Well, if you're sure," the other woman murmured uncertainly. Plastering an uneasy smile on her face, she reluctantly let go of her daughter's arm. "Go ahead, Mandy. The lady says it's okay."

The little girl eyed her mother doubtfully as if uncertain the nervous woman would change her mind. Her mother's smile wavered before becoming firmer as she waved encouragingly. "Go ahead, baby."

Mandy's face lit up and she turned to race over to where the other children were playing. Krono turned just as the little girl arrived, his nostrils flaring to sniff at her before his long tongue swiped over her in a friendly manner before laying his massive head on his front paws.

Mandy's mother let out the breath she was holding and smiled her first genuine smile. "Okay, this is good. Mandy needed this."

"All the little ones need it," Josie agreed, her own face cracked wide with a grin. She hooted with laughter when one of the kids went tumbling down Krono's long back. Terri laughed as well at the antics of the children until she wept tears of mirth. The laughter felt good. She couldn't remember the last time she had laughed so much. She had laughed with Veral from time to time over the last several days, but not the gut-busting laughter she was enjoying now.

From the corner of her eye, she saw Veral exit from the hallway, his eyes searching for her. His posture relaxed when he saw that she was merely having a good time. Then he stilled when he caught sight of Krono. Shaking his head, he chuffed and crouched in one corner to finish packing their bags with some of the supplies that had been brought out earlier to tend to the women.

Terri dismissed any of her worries from earlier when it came to the other women and enjoyed watching the children play throughout the late afternoon while she chatted with Josie. Until Lacey approached her with a nervous smile. Josie frowned from where she sat but Terri sighed. If she made a show of not being approachable, then the other girls would be afraid to come to her if they needed anything. All the social niceties were wearing thin.

Planting a stiff smile on her face, Terri addressed her politely. "Yes, Lacey? What can I do for you?"

The girl smiled cautiously, looking at her with an apparent sweetness from beneath her lashes. "Actually, you can. I need to go out and relieve myself, but it's starting to get dark, and I was wondering if I could borrow Veral to stand guard. It won't take long."

Terri's eyebrows shot up at the request, her eyes sliding over to Josie who gave her a distinct *"I told you so"* look. Clearing her throat, she attempted to deal with Lacey reasonably. "You want... Veral... to accompany you? Why don't you ask some of the other girls to go with you?"

Lacey shook her head, a petulant pout forming on her face. "No one else needs to go. I *need* Veral with me."

"I really don't think that's a good idea..." Terri attempted to explain but before she could even get the words out, Lacey went from sweet to arrogant. Terri risked a glance at Veral and sighed with relief. He hadn't noticed. There was little doubt in her mind that if he'd caught Lacey making any sort of threatening expression toward her that he would have hauled her out into the street and left her there. If he didn't kick her ass the entire way.

"Whatever," Lacey cut her off with a scornful, quiet hiss. Terri was just glad she was keeping her voice low so they weren't attracting attention. "You just don't want him to be alone with me because you're scared and jealous. Well, you should be. Unlike you, I'm the sort of real woman that a powerful man... uhm... male... would desire. He may have been stuck with you, but now that there are other women to choose from, he has options. You know that any man would prefer this over *that*."

Terri's mouth dropped open at her sheer gall. Even Josie beside her sputtered in disbelief. If Lacey truly believed that, she was going to be in for a huge disappointment. Terri wasn't above letting the woman learn some humility the hard way.

Rocking back a little, Terri's lips twisted and parted in a sharkish grin. "I'll tell you what. Just to prove to you how unthreatened I am, you go right ahead and ask him to accompany you with my blessing."

Lacey's dark eyes blinked in surprise, but it was fleeting.

"I'll do that," she challenged.

"A word of warning," Terri offered magnanimously. "Whatever you do, do not touch him. He won't be pleased if you do."

Lacey smiled smugly as she tossed her mass of tangled brown hair over her shoulder and strode over to Veral. Terri smirked as she watched but hoped that she wouldn't disregard her warning.

"What in the world are you thinking?" Josie whispered from where she was now perched behind Terri's shoulder. "You're really going to allow him to go off with her?" Terri's smirk widened into a fierce grin.

"Oh, I'm not worried about that. Just watch. She's about to have a rude awakening."

Terri's grin widened as Lacey sidled up to Veral. He was bent over the packs that they would be taking in when they raided the Reaper encampment. Terri had no doubt that he knew that the woman was behind from the way his back stiffened, but he was studiously ignoring her. Lacey, clearly not one to be snubbed, leaned forward and said something that Terri couldn't make out. Veral didn't even glance up, but a forbidding look crossed his face and his lips thinned before forming the shape of the simple response that Terri knew was coming. "No." His vibrissae snapped in emphasis before he dismissed Lacey altogether.

Lacey stared at him, her mouth gaping open and Josie chuckled. "Hopefully that will teach the girl something."

Terri nodded in agreement, but her smile slipped off her face as she watched Lacey scowl in their direction and step closer to Veral. She smirked and leaned forward, her breast brushing him suggestively as she touched his arm with one hand. Veral froze, his vibrissae lifting off his neck, rattling.

"Oh, shit!" Terri barked as she bolted to her feet and into the crowd of women. "I didn't think she would be that stupid."

"That twit," Josie huffed as she crossed her arms. "I wouldn't rescue her!" she shouted after her.

"Yeah, not an option!" she yelled back as she scooted between women, attempting to get to Lacey.

She knew that she was too late to intervene when Veral's vibrissae whipped fiercely. He spun around angrily on the woman intruding into his space. Gradually rising to his full height, easily three hundred and fifty pounds of pissed off alien turned on the human, his mandibles clicking in agitation. He stepped forward then, his vibrissae whipping through the air, daring anyone to get too close. Terri watched as his chest puffed out and a rattling growl rose into the air as his mandibles widened and snapped shut several times. Lacey paled as she scrambled backward. He loomed over her, his hands fisting tightly at his side.

"Do not seek such familiarity with me," he snarled just before his mandibles spread wide accompanied by a hellish roar. She screamed as a stream of urine trickled down her leg, soaking the floor. He gave her a disgusted look and turned away.

With a contemptuous growl, he attempted to step away from her, but Lacey, in her panic, moved in the same direction and in consequence threw herself into the range of his maddened vibrissae. Terri snagged the girl by the collar and pulled her to safety just in time, the vibrissae harmlessly snapping in the air while Veral backed away, still growling as he put distance between them.

Despite the fact that she hadn't been harmed, Lacey screamed uncontrollably as if she were being murdered. Terri rolled her eyes at the other woman's melodramatics. From how tightly he'd been clenching his fists, Veral obviously held back his instinctive impulse to maim the source of an uninvited touch until he managed to get away from her. Though he'd held back and refrained from harming the idiot, Terri knew that the entire episode was likely to impact the way the others saw him. They were already afraid of him and were only just starting to relax around his shadowy presence.

Lacey made matters worse as she continued to scream and stumbled away like a wounded animal with every eye in the room on her. Everyone fell silent until all that could be heard was her hysterical cries. A few of the girls bolted for cover, while several of the young women she'd been sitting near ran to her side, fussing over her dramatically.

The rest of the women didn't so much as move except to raise their eyebrows and turn away while they continued their quiet discussions. She could feel the weight of Josie's gaze on her and knew that she needed to explain a few things so that the woman could do damage control. She put it on her mental checklist as she followed her mate's continuous growl as he retreated rapidly from the women into the night. It didn't take long for the blubbering whimpers to die, but Terri wasn't paying attention. She ignored the hysterics as she approached Veral. His blazing eyes pierced her, his blue and silver gaze roaming over her face as his body continued to tremble with pent up aggression. The silver cybernetics stamped into his skin flared in the dark.

Running her hands over his arms and chest, she whispered to him as he struggled to regain control. Bit by bit, he slowly de-escalated, though the fury didn't completely drain out of his eyes and his body showed signs of continuing stress and aggression in the way he moved and held himself. The ceaseless rattle of his growl further emphasized his duress. Despite everything, he was unfailingly gentle with her as he gathered her into his arms, his body quivering against hers with unspoken need.

Tenderly, he dropped his forehead against hers and rumbled, "Anastha."

Terri tugged at the horn on his wrist. He needed to get outside and away from the other women so he could cool down. "Come on, big guy. Let's go outside and walk off some of that aggression."

He rumbled again and fell into step with her as they eased around the broken edge of a wall and into the street. They didn't make it far before his mood shifted as they neared the gaping wall of a house next door. He broke free of her hold, his hands banding around her waist as he pulled her against him and ducked around the corner into the strange building. Terri's breath left her in a rush of surprise.

"Veral?" she whispered.

He growled deep in his chest as his luminous eyes found her in the dark. "Trust me," he purred through his mandibles. "I need you."

"All right," she whispered. "I'm right here. You have me—all of me."

Dropping his head, Veral dragged in deep, shaky breaths as if he was still just barely keeping his rage under control. "I have never hurt a female in anger but, for the first time, I wanted to. I couldn't bear her touch on me. I was clear that I had no interest in accompanying her or being in her company, yet she persisted... she dared to touch me." He sounded so sickened by the entire thing that Terri's heart lurched in sympathy, her arms coming around him.

"It's over now," she whispered. "I'm so sorry. I sent her to teach her a lesson because she was being rude when I didn't give her what she wanted. I warned her not to touch you, though. I shouldn't have said anything. Maybe it never would have occurred to her if she hadn't felt like she had something to prove to me. She desired your protection."

Veral snarled and clicked his mandibles irritably. "Many of those females, the weepy ones, are too weak to survive outside of the protection of their males. They are dependent on those bonds not only for fulfillment but also for safety. They would be better served to arrive at the coast quickly and surrender themselves into the care of whatever city they find there. They are not strong enough to be the mate of a trader, a salvager, a warrior, or any Argurma at all. I am fortunate that I found you. If we were separated, you would survive without me if necessary," he murmured, running his nose through her hair. "You would curse me in your human way, but you would remain strong until we were reunited. You are a most worthy mate."

Terri stifled a silly smile and held him for several minutes. She didn't argue with him, though she wasn't so sure that she wouldn't have at least some hysterics if she got separated from him in a dangerous situation. But she liked the image that he painted of her. She liked how he saw her. When his breath huffed evenly against her neck, she pulled back and looked up at him with amusement. "Better now?"

"No," he bit out, pushing his pelvis against her belly. "The aggression won't just go away in my species. It needs to be worked out of my system by giving it a method of releasing energy. I can go hunt to take my anger out on prey… or…"

"Or?" she breathed, her pulse racing with the first flush of excitement.

"I will not deny that more pleasure and expediency can be found expending my passions in the arms of my mate," he rumbled. "We have much that needs to be done tonight. I would much rather satisfy it this way." He paused, his gaze searching her as his mandibles expanded and his nostrils flared. "You desire it too. My systems detect your increased heart rate, your body temperature climbing with your arousal. Your pupils are marginally dilated. Will you accept my rage?"

"Oh, fuck yes," she whispered, excitement churning within her as her mate held her despite the power in his cybernetic parts and system.

He sank down into the sand with her, stripping off their armor with inhuman speed as they went. Dipping his arms behind her legs, he lifted her bottom up into his lap as his extruded cock searched for her. It slipped across her damp sex only once before plunging deep within her.

Terri bit back a startled cry, not wishing to alarm the other women so close by. She shifted one of his large hands over her mouth with a meaningful look. He stared at her in confusion before his lips quirked and he nodded in understanding.

Holding her tight, he muffled her cries as he pounded down into her canted pelvis. Though far more aggressive, Terri welcomed and loved every bit of it. The tips of his claws raked with more pressure against her hips and thighs. His cock claimed her at an almost punishing tempo and depth with every thrust. Terri met each thrust, whimpering and panting, demanding more. She dragged her own nails down his scaled sides, eliciting suppressed, throaty moans of pleasure for her efforts. This time when he spilled his seed it came abruptly, sending them both over the edge — without implantation. He hadn't in the bath either, she realized only now.

Panting, she glanced up at him as he lowered her hips to the ground. "You didn't implant this time or when we bathed."

He shook his head. "As long as my seed is within you and your body is attempting to hold it, my hormone levels do not spike enough for my body to implant."

"Can your system control your hormones enough to prevent implantation?"

Veral paused thoughtfully. "I don't know," he said at last. "I can program my hormones to remain at a steady level but, given that you are my mate, I do not know if they will be instinctually altered in response to the scent of your arousal, the heat of your sex surrounding mine, or any of the other variables that occur during copulation. It is something worth trying in the future."

"Sounds like a plan," she said as she stretched languidly. "Mind handing me my pants, my love? I need to speak to Josie and do some damage control before all the women start tip-toeing around you like they expect you to freak out. We need some ground rules, I think."

18

"As far as I can tell from when I was here last time, they're keeping the women in that building there," Terri leaned in to whisper as she gestured to the lone gray-walled building. It was completely covered with graffiti, half of which was distinctly pornographic. "I do know that women aren't allowed free run of the camp. A woman I know, Meg, willingly joined them to be kept under their protection."

Veral froze, his head canting to the side. "Meg." He said the name slowly. "I believe I know of this female of whom you speak. She was very frightened when her male—Dale—brought her to their commander." Veral's eyes slid away to sweep over the torch-lit camp stretched out before them. "I was curious as to what may have happened to the female."

Terri grimaced. That had been the subject of a number of her arguments with Meg. Guiltily she wondered how her friend was fairing. She hadn't seen her out in days, not since fleeing with Veral. She suddenly felt like a really shitty friend.

"Dale is an asshole," she said, "but Meg won't leave his side, no matter how much I beg her. I don't know if he has her brainwashed or if she is just *that* scared of what could be done to her without his protection. She sees her submission to him as the only thing keeping her safe. Still, she's told me a lot about how things work in the camp. That's how I know as much as I do."

"From what she said, those who have some sort of arrangement or an established relationship with the guys are allowed to remain within their tents rather than in the little whorehouse where the men share them. Whoreshack, really," she observed in distaste. "The women we're looking for will likely be confined in there. I doubt any of them will have had the opportunity to find a 'protector' among the guys here. *Protector*." She couldn't resist sneering in disgust. "That said, I'm sure the women inside would tell us if someone got separated from them. I hope," she amended, thinking of the behavior of some of the women she'd been taking care of.

Crouched at her side, Veral grunted as he narrowed his glowing eyes at the building and gave a sharp nod. It was more of a dip of his square chin, but his eyes gleamed as he focused on their target from where they were perched on a nearby rise. They were high enough up that they could easily see inside the compound from above. The silver in Veral's eyes brightened as he stared down at the building.

"My systems show several human lifeforms in that building," he said, his vibrissae puffing out around him with the focus of his scrutiny.

She stared at them and frowned. Normally she loved his vibrissae, but when they were displayed like that it made them a much clearer target in the moonlight. She coughed. "Excellent. Umm, Veral, maybe you should bind your vibrissae so they don't attract attention," she suggested.

Veral shook his head. "I depend on them too much for protection and information. Binding them would be both dangerous and foolhardy." His lips quirked in amusement, though he obviously worked to restrain himself as his mandibles twitched several times. "Do not worry, anastha. They will be kept close to my body in hunting mode when we are within the Reaper territory unless I am forced to defend us."

"Okay," she replied, blushing at his explanation. Of course he wouldn't have them out waving around. Even when he attacked the Reapers in the desert, his vibrissae had remained close to him, making his fighting silhouette more streamlined and lethal until he was upon his victim. He definitely hadn't needed her to tell him to keep them pulled in.

"Awesome... Yeah. We've got this then," she said as she cleared her throat, her acute discomfort making her fill in the silence with awkward, fumbling words. Why was she suddenly acting like a fool? It had to be the pressure and the adrenaline running through her.

Veral reached out and stroked her cheek gently. Terri sighed as she leaned into his touch, taking pleasure from the weight of his hand. Even his eyes lingering on her features was reassuring. his lips curving sweetly as he looked down upon her. She stared up at him, caught up in the raw, naked emotion in his eyes. It was a startling change from the way he usually appeared, and it totally captivated her and pulled her in.

There was still a hardness to his gaze, but she knew that softness was only for her. It was only because he looked upon her.

Leaning forward, he bumped the broad ridge of his nose against hers in a silent expression of affection before he pulled away and dropped quietly off the side of the rise.

Terri scooted forward in the sand, grateful for the armor. Without it, she would have been wincing painfully from the rock and fine granules sifting into her shirt... Not to mention checking for venomous passengers hopping a ride. Glancing over the edge at her mate waiting below, she allowed herself to drop down into his waiting arms.

They crept through the dark, making their way to the perimeter wall. It was just as gruesome as before, maybe more with the added decay, but at least Terri didn't need to linger this time. They weren't waiting for anyone to let them in. One of Veral's arms wrapped around her seconds before he leaped to the top of the wall. The movement was so quick that Terri swallowed back an instinctive yelp. He clung to the wall with the claws of his opposite hand before he dropped onto the other side, flattening them to the ground.

Terri, pinned beneath him, held her breath, her ears straining for any sign of someone nearing as Veral crouched over her. His weight pressed her close to the ground, enough so that she was certain that she would hear footfalls if anyone so much as walked their way. From the corner of her eye, she saw that his ears pricked up, listening for approaching threats as his glowing eyes scanned the area around them. Once satisfied that they were in the clear, he eased away to let her up. Standing slowly, he helped her to feet. A scream rent the night air, startling them both. Veral spun in place, his vibrissae flaring as his hand twitched as if he were going to snatch her up again. His head tilting, he looked down at her in consideration.

Terri pressed a flattened palm against his chest. "Nuh-uh. I won't go back, not until I've done what I've come here to do. So don't even think of throwing me back over that wall," she whispered fiercely.

"I can retrieve them," he growled. "You don't need to be here. I object most strenuously to this."

"We've discussed this. They aren't going to just come to you, Veral. Remember, humans are frightened of you… It's that whole not cuddly thing you have going on. They're more likely to accept help from me."

"Then they are foolish," he grunted irritably, though he smirked at her description of him as if it were a compliment. "I am a highly evolved bio-cybernetic being. My nanos alone, that I've had since birth, make me a far more efficient organism. There is none better equipped to rescue them than me. Not cuddly works in my favor for destroying their enemies. That is what is necessary."

"Okay, but that doesn't do a damn bit of good when it comes to reasoning with frightened women. This is how we have to do it, whether you like it or not."

Veral's eyes narrowed in response but he didn't argue further with her. He looked extremely displeased but nodded. Instead, he moved forward with purpose. He didn't leave her to follow after him but nudged her with his arm to keep her by his side as they made their way through the encampment, staying well out of the way of the lights scattered through the vicinity.

As expected, they encountered no one as they made their way from the nearest perimeter wall to the shed. On her first trip through the compound, she'd noted that the behavior of the Reapers erred closer to anarchy than organization. This worked to their advantage, since there was absolutely no order to the camp itself, leaving it open and vulnerable. As before, all the tents were practically clustered on top of each other at one end, leaving much of it unsupervised and in complete darkness other than a few areas with torches. One such spot was the area directly around the shed, but this was also the case throughout the camp around the bonfires where food cooked and drink ran freely.

Though every gang member hung around those areas informally, there were no guards keeping watch. Terri had come to suspect that the Reapers depended on their reputation to keep intruders out, and the lack of order to confuse strangers and new recruits. Even the men standing around the shed seemed to be there more by chance rather than with a purpose. Not one of them was paying any attention to anything coming at them from the dark recesses of the compound.

In the light of the torches set around the shack, Terri was able to get a good look at the group of men who were standing around outside of it. To her surprise, not just one or two, but the majority of them, had obvious signs of mutations. Few looked anything close to normal, though all were incredibly dirty. She wondered how much of a role those most obviously mutated played in hunting down women. Their skills were likely put to use in other ways that she didn't want to think about.

In the case of many of the men, their skin hung from warped bone and muscle. One of the men even had an additional set of eye sockets pitted lower beneath his cheekbones, sealed over with skin. She had never had the opportunity to study the Reapers too closely, but more than half seemed affected. Nauseating green pus dripped from more than one orifice. Was this solely the result of the mutations brought on by nuclear fallout in blast areas, or was a portion of it linked to generations of rampant cannibalism and other savage acts? She'd heard rumors about inbreeding and disease but didn't know what to believe. Now she wasn't so sure. With this new information, she doubted that they were a recently established gang, given their size. No doubt their mutated daddies and granddaddies had been eating people and breeding their lineage long before the current power took control.

"There are more signs of strange polymorphisms among your species in these males as well," Veral also observed. "They appear varied from minor to severe cases."

"I didn't realize... I didn't know that there were so many mutations," she whispered. "I knew that the war created some—like that guy we came across when salvaging—but I always assumed it was in small, isolated cases. I never imagined it would be anything like this."

"Mutation will spread uncontrollably where it is given free rein." His thick, horned brow furrowed. "In my species, there has recently been a substantial increase in offspring born with violet eyes. It is a strange mutation that was first documented one thousand, seven hundred and twenty-five planetary revolutions ago, and yet when I left, the cases were spreading in the hundreds. Adults were discovered to be genetic carriers for the mutation due to early unregulated breeding practices before the Council began licensing mating and breeding. No doubt some of these males possessing the less severe mutations would be able to create thriving offspring that could potentially benefit your species were it not for their depravity," Veral observed.

Not for the first time, his impartial, almost cold description of the fate of her species left Terri feeling aghast. Whatever affections he felt toward her, they did not extend to her species.

"You're saying that the mutations are a good thing?" she whispered vehemently.

Her mate gave her a calculated glance before returning his gaze to the shelter. "They can be when they are not errors in the genetic coding. Some mutations would also be in response to the drastic environmental changes you have noted in your world. I calculate the odds are in favor of the rescued females suffering minor biological mutations that allow them to carry offspring to term where others are failing, by your admission. In cases of mutagenesis, it occurs in response to environmental factors for which the current biology may lack. Many of the Argurma would like to eradicate mutations, missing the point entirely that certain mutations would be a positive evolutionary growth for our species. The violet eyes in my species are linked to a natural reduction in a chemical that not only provides a certain pigment to my species, making the scales thinner and also paler in color, but lowers our core temperatures. Some believe that it is in response to the growing heat on our planet from our suns. Regardless of the cause of a mutation, no species can stay static forever. They must change and adapt in order to flourish."

Terri considered this. He had a valid observation—up to a point. "I'm not so sure I see the results of the mutations here very favorably," she whispered.

"No, I would not classify these males as ones that I would wish to continue their line," Veral said. His attention shifted to the males she was watching. A puzzled frown pulled at his mouth and his nostrils flared only to be followed by a look of disgust.

"That smell… It is vizi!" he growled as he drew up a flap of material around the neck of his armor and pulled it over his mouth and nose.

She wrinkled her nose as the sickening smell drifted over to her. Terri couldn't blame him. She didn't have a strong sense of smell and it was nauseating even to her. A few among the men nearest to them leaned on the wall as they smoked sticky sap from the Orange-Bloom. The flower had appeared about fifty years ago and the sap not only caused a euphoric high but was extremely addictive. The way the smokers were leaning against the wall, smiling in the far distance, she had no doubt that their eyes were glazed over with the effects of the sap.

"Those humans are behaving abnormally, and not only because they do not seem to notice the abominable smell. Their bodily chemicals appear imbalanced," Veral observed.

She chuckled. "They're 'higher than a kite,' as my grandmother was fond of saying." She frowned. "I don't know what a kite is. Maybe some kind of bird? Either way, it's a drug to make them feel good."

"It is foolish to intentionally induce impairment to one's functions," Veral stated, although a hint of humor edged his tone as they continued to watch for their opening.

"Let me guess," she said, her attention trained on the pair of men laughing and slipping an item between each other in front of the door, "there are no drugs on Argurumal."

Now the male beside her snorted derisively. "Do not be absurd. There are drugs on nearly every planet in intergalactic space. Some planets are cultivated exclusively for the addictive drugs they produce. The Argurma are no less susceptible to their influence, but most of the warrior and trader classes have cybernetic augments that make such impulses less likely since we have a more logical core processing unit. Even still among the general population, due to cybernetics, only cases of severe emotional imbalance will drive a cybernetically enhanced Argurma to seek such an escape."

Veral slipped forward to the right, shifting his angle of vision. She squinted through the darkness searching for him but became disoriented when a raucous sound rose from the center of the camp. It was loud enough that it made Terri jump, her heart pounding in her chest.

After several minutes, Veral scooted back to her side, his face inches from hers as he spoke. "Most of the males are pulling away from the building. I suspect it has something to do with the infernal noise among those gathering in the center of the compound." He tilted his head, appearing to listen. "They are angry about their losses from their latest hunt, but more so since so many females escaped them."

Terri frowned and strained to hear. To her frustration, she didn't hear anything like that but knew that Veral's hearing was likely far superior to her own even before it had been enhanced.

"All right, let's go," she whispered as she patted her bag. "Once we get the females out, I have a nasty surprise for the assholes."

A bony brow arched at her, and she grinned savagely as she opened her pack. A few days ago, during one of their salvages, she had found an entire box of explosive materials labeled "TNT." Veral hadn't been interested in it since it wasn't worth credits for him to collect, but Terri had been fascinated. It hadn't been difficult to work out how it was used, although Veral had glared at her when she'd set one off a bit too close to their salvaging area. Now his lips quirked, and glowing eyes narrowed with unmistakable satisfaction. Her alien sure did like his destruction and violence, but unlike the Reapers, he was tempered by mercy and logic about how and when he used it.

At Veral's signal, she dropped back, her body tensing with anticipation.

19

*T*erri wiped her sweaty palms on the legs of her armor, the oddly absorbent material drawing in the moisture. She was nervous, but she knew what to do—though she almost wished they brought Krono with them rather than leaving him to guard the women. She would have felt better having him nearby. She suspected Veral would have too since he'd protested leaving the dorashnal behind. She'd insisted on leaving protection, however. It had been the right decision, but that didn't mean that she couldn't regret it on some level.

Veral turned and gave her a questioning look, no doubt sensing her anxiety. She smiled at him and gave him a thumbs-up. His eyes focused on the gesture for a long minute before he nodded and slunk away

She was fine.

Terri had to hang back while he approached the shack. Veral had insisted on it, claiming that it would be more expedient and efficient for him to deal with killing the Reapers. Her task was to keep the women calm and escort them out of the compound.

Terri had no argument with that. She wasn't trained to fight and had little instinct for killing anything. She didn't even own a single weapon after losing her baseball bat while fleeing from the

Reapers. That didn't stop her from admiring the way he silently crept up behind one of the nearest men. With a quick twist of Veral's arm, he broke the Reaper's neck before the man could make a sound.

Veral continued to move like a wraith around them, picking them off one by one. The Reapers, deep in their own fog of drug-induced bliss, weren't aware of what hit them. It was, in Terri's opinion, far more merciful than they deserved, but the goal was silence rather than mercy so she had no real complaint.

As Veral took care of the last one, Terri opened the door slowly so that the hinges only squeaked minimally, and stepped inside. Immediately, she gagged at the overwhelming odor of piss, shit, the sour musk of unwashed bodies, and the unmistakable odor of sex. Her eyes widened in horror. There had to have been fifty women crammed into the small space. They were huddled together, filthy, and several had open sores and wounds that had been left untreated.

As her eyes scanned the crowd, she recognized a handful pressed into one corner as those who had been captured during the caravan raid. They held small children close to them. One cried over a little girl whose skin was tinged blue, her glassy eyes staring sightlessly. Her tiny body must have been brutalized and returned to her mother.

Terri felt her throat close in grief and wanted to shut her eyes against the horrors of the prison.

One of the caravan women cried out upon seeing her, and the sound was soon echoed as they pushed through the other women to get to her. The other women turned their heads, tears of relief streaming from their eyes as they too surged toward her. Terri waved her hands frantically to silence them, and the noise dropped so quickly that she blinked in surprise until she felt a familiar presence behind her.

Turning her head, she saw Veral standing just behind her. Every woman went silent. Unlike those women who Terri and Veral had saved, all the women collectively gravitated toward the alien. Terri gaped at them before feeling a surprising wave of irritation as they began to press in around him with sounds of gratitude, more than one woman whispering, begging them to take her with him. Terri bit back a snarl and shook her head in an effort to clear it.

These women were traumatized. She had no reason to be jealous.

Clearing her throat to get their attention, she stepped forward and spoke in a low, urgent voice. "Don't be afraid. We're getting you out of here. Everyone needs to quietly follow me out of the building and stick together. Does anyone need help?"

A woman toward the back hesitantly held up her hand. The women parted before her, several of the women from the caravan looking on anxiously, many of them with tears in their eyes. Terri approached, and her eyes misted over as she saw the woman seated on a stool, half of her leg missing above the knee. A blood-soaked tourniquet was wrapped around the stump. The woman managed a weak smile despite her obvious pain.

"Yeah, I don't think I'm going to be able to walk out of here. They cut it off when I tried to escape," she whispered. Her face was pale and drawn but she met Terri's eyes steadily, her lips set firmly against the pain. Her expression struck a familiar chord with Terri as the woman bit out, "I took one of the bastards out though. Gutted him like a fish with his own knife."

Terri leaned forward, trying to determine the best way to move the woman. "I don't suppose you're related to Josie?"

The other woman barked out a surprised laugh, wincing when it brought her pain, but her eyes contained a spark of amusement and relief when she met Terri's eyes. "I should say so. I'm her daughter, Becky. Mom made it… Thank the gods! I'm so fucking happy to hear it," she gasped. "I wouldn't mind seeing her again if it's all the same. Am I going to be able to get out of here?"

Terri winced. "Yeah… One sec, okay? Veral, come here," she hissed, knowing full well that he would be able to hear her.

The women parted before him as Veral made his way over to

her side, his churning vibrissae the only sign of his obvious dislike in response to the human women pressing in so close around him. At least they were only crowding him a little. No one made any attempt to touch him. Terri stiffened but then stifled a laugh as one of the women attempted to lean against him and he side-stepped her with an irritated huff. He didn't seem overly concerned about the injured woman, although his eyes did narrow perceptively.

"Becky here needs help. The Reapers took her leg after she killed one of them in her attempt to escape," she murmured to him in a low voice. Veral nodded as he hummed with approval. The sound was one of grudging admiration for the wounded woman, but he gave Terri a sideways glance of displeasure.

"Do you wish me to carry her? I will not be efficient at protecting the females if I am carrying one." He sounded pained at the idea, but the fact that he offered to touch the woman if Terri required it, despite his natural repulsion toward physical contact, made her smile.

"I think it will be better if your hands were free," she whispered. She didn't miss the relieved expression that flitted across his features. "I have an idea. Let me have one of the collector carts. It may be big enough for Becky to fit inside." She gave Becky an apologetic look. "It'll be a bit uncomfortable to ride, but I think it's probably our best option."

"Works for me." Becky groaned. "I'm already in pain. What's a little more? As long as I can get the fuck out of here, I'm game."

Veral smiled approvingly. "You would make a fine mate for any warrior. I am mated... so another warrior," he clarified sternly.

Becky's eyebrows shot up. "Okay... umm, thanks. I think." She looked to Terri for confirmation. "That was a compliment, right? I just can't tell with men anymore, much less what appears to be an alien. Very freaky, by the way. I would be screaming in terror, as would the rest of them, if they weren't so damn happy to be rescued."

Terri smiled and patted the other woman's arm. "The best kind of compliment coming from him," she assured her. Turning away, Terri held her hand out for the disc.

Veral jerked his chin down and unfastened the disc from his belt, tossing it to the ground behind them. With a finger pressed on his wristband, the device immediately deployed, expanding into a collector cart amid the gasps of the women watching. Without preamble, he bent down, picked up the injured woman, and deposited her in the cart.

Terri opened her mouth to thank him but jerked in surprise when he grabbed ahold of her arm and yanked her toward him. Rubbing his cheek and mandible against the side of her face, he took her hand in his, turning her arm as his fingers traced out a pattern. The area he touched lit up with a dim flash. His thumb caressed her arm once before he released her.

"What is that?" she asked him quietly.

"The beacon for the collector cart. You will now lead the females out as we agreed. It will follow you at whatever pace you set. You know where to go. I will meet you at our shelter."

Her brow furrowed. "This isn't how we planned it. We're supposed to leave together after I set the dynamite around the shack. What are you planning to do?" she asked.

In answer, he pulled her bag from her shoulder, removing her emergency supplies and setting them on the ground. His own bag he set on the ground beside hers and transferred the supplies to it. Lifting his bag back up, he slid the straps over her arms, tightening them with a flick of his wrists. He trilled in satisfaction as he picked up her bag and looped it over his own shoulder. He pulled the strap tight around the hard, protruding bone and thick muscle mass.

"I will destroy them," he said simply and then promptly turned and walked out of the shack.

The women immediately began to whisper in a panic.

"Where's he going?"

"I thought he was here to save us!"

"Why is he leaving without us?"

"What are we going to do without him to protect us?"

"Quiet!" Terri hissed. "Veral *is* protecting us. He's going to provide a distraction and hopefully take some Reapers out in the process. My mate will meet back up with us when he's done. We will survive just fine. There are no posted guards, and the Reapers are busy further in the compound. I'll take you to the shelter, where those of you from the caravan can be reunited with your families and friends. We've got clean water there and can tend to your wounds."

"You can't protect us," one of the women complained.

Terri felt her patience fading. "We're going to protect ourselves. We are *not* new to this world. We're survivors," she snarled quietly.

Some of the women made noises of agreement, though many, especially among the most abused women who'd been captives of the gang for far longer, looked around with uncertainty.

As she threaded her way through the women, Terri stopped and rested a hand on the shoulder of the grieving mother who still clung to her daughter. "We have to go now," Terri whispered, her heart going out to her.

"I can't leave her…" the woman sobbed quietly.

"She's already gone. She's with you in the only way she can be right now, and she wouldn't want you to die. You can't risk being slowed down by carrying her."

"I want to die. I don't want to outlive my child. They should have taken and killed *me*. Not my little girl."

Terri's eyes misted and she swiped at her eyes with the back of her hand as she looked down at her. "Please," she whispered. "Come with us. I promise I'll get you to the coast and I will see to it that you are provided with a small memorial for her. It's better than dying here with her. Live on, and remember her."

The woman swallowed and reluctantly nodded as she tenderly lowered the little girl to the ground. A small group of women surrounded her, their hands touching her shoulder in reassurances, murmuring comforting words as if they'd done so numerous times to soothe each other. She leaned into them, melding among their number.

Glancing around, Terri spoke quietly. "Let's move out."

With minimal hushed complaints, the captured females fell in behind her. Becky reclined in the collector cart and gave her a weak smile and a thumbs-up even as she panted around her pain. To Terri's disbelief, she was the only one who seemed entirely cooperative with her efforts. The others followed reluctantly, searching for Veral, motivated only by the desire to not be left behind rather than confidence in Terri to lead them to safety. The collector cart shifted forward as Terri stepped away from the group of women, its wheels rolling soundlessly as they filed out of the building.

20

*V*eral stood as a silent sentinel on top of the strange cell as he watched Terri lead the women out and across the compound. His fingers twitched with a desire to take Terri and put distance between them and the females. He hadn't cared for the way they had pressed in close around him, their overpowering desire to cling to him suffocating him. He thought he had been irritated before with the ceaseless wailing and frightened screams of the females from the caravan, but at least then the females were not tempted to touch him like these were.

His skin still itched with distaste and his vibrissae snapped angrily in the air as he recalled how close some of them had come to leaning against him. Before Terri had called out to him, he had warned more than one female off by flaring his mandibles. Even that hadn't been a foolproof deterrent. It was only due to his commitment to Terri and his oath given to her that he tolerated it.

Veral growled as his processors rejected the assessment. He was unable to lie to himself and claim that it was merely the commitment of their mate bonding. He felt genuine affection for his female. Everything within him was tied to her, even the very heart of him.

While she'd been aboard his ship sleeping, he ran through the downloaded catalogs of information he recovered from the satellites, looking for any information pertaining to human mating. He saw odd rituals involving offerings of flowers and glossy brown pellets, and even jewels. He understood jewels, as Argurma males and females both often presented gifts of jewels to celebrate triumphs and honors, but it was odd to see it as part of mating courtship. Then he finally arrived at the concept of love.

As he watched his mate strike out, the longing in his heart told him what he instinctively knew, contrary to all programming that should have overridden such a malfunction beyond what would be considered healthy attachment to a mate.

His heart belonged to her. Every affection and devotion was hers.

Terri made him *feel* and made him remember glimpses of buried memories and sensations from long ago.

There would never be a Veral without Terri by his side. He loved her.

As soon as the last female cleared the compound, he bared his teeth with a silent snarl as he turned toward the communal fires. He would deal with the Reapers and make it quick so he could hasten back to his mate. Though his people would consider his processors malfunctioning, he ignored any calculations that suggested it would be more expedient to rain terror on the camp with his own hands. Although he desired it, thirsted to cause panic within his enemies, he didn't want that fear to alert anyone to his mate's presence and that of the escaping females while they were still in the confines of the compound. Instead, he kept to the deep shadows, out of the reach of the torches, as he crept nearer to the central fires.

He paused as a pair of humans blundered into the torchlight just in front of him. He recognized them at once. Dale, stinking of fermented grain and sweat, dragged a familiar dark-haired female. Veral cocked his head, his mandibles working in a rare show of indecision firing through his processors. He wanted to hurry into the heart of the camp with his mate's "gift" where it would do far more good than if it were set around the structure where she'd planned to place it. Yet he was hard-pressed to pass up the opportunity to destroy one of the males who'd held him captive.

Clicking in anticipation, Veral made his decision. He would kill the male quickly, though not so much that he didn't get some sort of satisfaction from the male's pain and terror. *Then* he would complete his task.

Satisfied, he crept closer.

"Come on! Hurry up, would ya? For fuck's sake, Meg, I don't know why you're dragging your feet about this. We're going to grab a couple more of the girls for a bit of fun and join Marcus after he's done with some business."

"You know I don't know like it when Marcus joins us," Meg complained in a small voice.

"Fuck, you are always complaining. Maybe I should trade you in for one of the new girls like some of the guys have been saying. You are my whore—you don't get to voice an opinion. I've told you countless times. Do you really need me to beat it into you again?" he snarled. "Now look, you're ruining my buzz, so shut your hole. Crazy fucking bitch."

"I'm sorry, Dale," she whispered meekly in reply.

Veral growled loud enough to be heard as he drew closer. He wanted to smell the fear pouring off the male. Dale stopped in his tracks, his eyes bulging as he looked around. Veral knew that the male couldn't see him… Not yet. His dual tongues stroked over his lips, his mandibles yawning wide, and he savored the flavor of the male's mounting distress as he growled louder and dashed by him so that Dale would feel the barest brush of the predator who hunted and toyed with him. Normally, Veral preferred to strike with speed and efficiency. It made sense to kill enemies emotion-lessly, without passions incited, but this male deserved to suffer for daring to chain him.

"W… what the fuck!?" Dale stuttered, his voice trembling. Veral bared his teeth in triumph, unseen.

"Dale?" Meg whispered as she attempted to step closer to the male.

"Fuck. *Fuck!* I told Marcus we should have found a way to get through the armor and scales and killed that motherfucking alien! I ain't dying for stupid shit. Sorry, darlin', looks like it's you or me. I enjoy living too much," Dale said, a sheen of sweat showing on his brow. Meg gaped at him as he gripped her arm and shoved her out ahead of him hard enough that she fell to the ground outside the circle of torchlight. "Take her, alien, she's all yours!" he hollered.

"Dale, you limp-dicked asshole!" Meg shrieked as she struggled to rise.

Veral didn't spare the woman a glance as he stepped over her legs and stalked toward the human male, his claws sliding down over his fingertips. Meg jerked as she sensed him move by her, whimpering as she drew her legs up to her body. Veral's attention could not be diverted from the male. Dale could have thrown credits at him if he'd possessed any and it wouldn't have done any good.

Veral's honor demanded satisfaction.

With a wide, terrible grin, Veral stepped out of the shadows, savoring the male's reaction. Dale shouted out a sound almost like a squeal of terror and backed away so quickly that he stumbled over his own feet and fell to the ground. Veral considered just how he would like to tear the human apart, his processors analyzing what would bring the most pain in the limited amount of time he was working with.

"Please, man, don't hurt me," Dale wheezed. "I gave you the bitch! Spare me, I beg you."

Veral hissed. "What do I want with your female?"

"Shit, you speak! I don't know... I don't even fucking care! Fuck her or eat her. Whichever you prefer. Just don't hurt me!"

Veral inhaled, his mandibles expanding as Dale's eyes grew rounder. "I remember you," he growled. I thought you scented familiar before... You hunted my mate."

"Fuck, your mate? I didn't know. I mean, hey, come on, it's all just pussy. If I accidentally did anything to hurt your... uh... mate, just take Meg. She's a good fuck. I promise. I'll be sad to have lost her."

"A good... fuck?" Veral sneered.

"Man, *please*. I'll do anything. Have mercy!"

"Like you have mercy on those who take, rape, and eat?" Veral queried, his mandibles rattling in time with his vibrissae as he tipped his head again thoughtfully. "You speak to the wrong one for mercy. My mate is not here." He chuffed cruelly. "The only thing you can do is die."

Veral surged forward, his claws slashing out as Dale screamed. The sound was cut short on a gurgle of blood, the male's body twitching as Veral bent down to look him in the eye, his claws buried in the male's throat as blood poured in gushing streams down his neck.

"Quiet," Veral hissed in irritation.

He held the human in place until the male fell forward. Stepping aside at the last minute to avoid contact, the sound of his claws slipping free from human flesh squelched loudly. He grimaced at the gore, but it could not be helped. He would clean them later.

Turning his head, his eyes searched out and found the human female cowering and she backed away. He stalked toward her with an impatient grunt.

"Please, I don't want to die!" she cried out.

He stopped a short distance from her. "Are you certain?"

"What? ...Yes, of course I'm certain!"

He rattled his mandibles in frustration. "Think of that before you make an alliance that could kill you," he spat out. His point made, he stepped back, away from her. She stared at him mutely.

"You're letting me go?"

"Would you like me to kill you instead?"

"No!" She looked away into the dark and bit her lip. "Do you think... could I stay with you?"

Veral growled in frustration. "Human females, always asking

for protection. No," he snapped. "I have a mate. Look for a worthy human male to take care of you."

She shrank. "Sorry."

"Do not be sorry," he muttered in exasperation. "My female would not like you to be sad or hurt. Terri is taking the other females to the gate. If you wish to find safety, I suggest you join them there."

"Terri is here?" the female gasped as she bolted to her feet. Her expression clouded with confusion. "Terri is your mate?"

He rumbled an affirmative and turned toward the fires burning in the near distance.

"Wait," Meg whispered urgently.

He cocked his head and twitched his mandibles.

"Marcus is up to something. I don't know what, but he hasn't been partying with the guys. Be careful, okay? If Terri mated with you, she must care for you a lot," she said softly. "I'm sorry I asked you to take me. I'm just… scared. She deserves a good guy."

Veral considered her thoughtfully. "I thank you for the warning and accept your apology. You are not a bad female. You are stronger than you look, I think," he said. "Find my anastha, my Terri, and leave this place."

She jerked her head in a hasty nod and fled in the direction of the gates. He didn't bother to stay and watch. A sense of urgency consumed him. He needed to get back to his mate… but first, the Reapers, as he promised.

With a growl, he sprung forward, racing through the shadows toward the firelight that seemed to mock him as it danced in the air. Something was not right.

21

*L*urking in the shadows beyond the edge of the fires, Veral searched the crowd dispassionately, his recorders once more engaged. He was recording for two reasons: to show his mate the glory of vanquishing of their enemies, and to preserve a record of the strange social phenomena exhibited before him. The riotous press of human males was an impressive sight. They practically climbed over each other in their frenzy, waving all manner of weapons from knives to crude spears to guns. A lone male close to the fire, who seemed to be encouraging the strange revelry, waved around Veral's blaster.

Although he hated to leave without his favored weapon, he wouldn't risk his mission for it. Terri was depending on him to wipe out this menace. It was not only logical to remove the blight from the city, but it would give him a great deal of satisfaction to do so. Veral never forgot and rarely forgave. As far as he was concerned, outside of the females, few were innocent. Everywhere he looked, he saw nothing but chaotic brutality. His gaze landed on a lone exception that drew his eye, the one point of stillness among the human frenzy.

A small cluster of human males—soft-faced, likely young and frightened—stood just off to the side, their bodies crowded together tightly as if attempting to draw strength from each other. Veral understood this behavior. He had seen its likeness on young males when they were led in for processing for the cybernetic implants upon reaching maturity.

These males were being forcibly conscripted into the unit.

He trilled quietly to himself, feeling the odd sensation of sympathy that flowed through him. He couldn't zero in on its cause, recognizing only a flicker of an undefinable memory he couldn't quite grasp. Before, he might have ignored such an impulse as a malfunction. But since bonding with his mate, he allowed himself to acknowledge the emotion and accept it. On a deep level, he understood the fear that quelled them. The choice between death and joining was a great motivator for increasing a unit's ranks. He wondered what they would do if presented with an opportunity to be free.

Compelled by the emotions stirred within him, he decided to find out. Perhaps he was feeling moved to exhibit this compassion his mate had spoken of. The idea didn't thrill him, but he felt like he was reclaiming a part of himself as he moved toward the youths.

Leaning into a crouch, Veral hugged the shadows as he closed the short distance that separated them. He slid behind one of the males lingering at the back and yanked him into the shadows, his hand clasped over the youth's mouth. The male's arms flailed, his body twisting as the stench of fear rose up from his pores. Veral tightened his arms around him, restricting his movement until the youth ceased moving, his breath coming out in soft, rapid pants.

Leaning forward, he whispered into the male's ear. "Do not speak or make a sound. Just indicate with the movement of your head, human. Do you want to escape this place?"

The male stiffened and remained unresponsive. Veral wagered that the human was debating whether or not he was being deceived. The quality was both admirable and annoying.

"This is no deception. You are wasting my time. Yes or no," he growled.

The male's head jerked in a positive response.

"Very well. You shall have the opportunity to earn it. Do the others also wish to depart?"

Again, he nodded.

"Return then to your companions and tell any whom you think wish to depart to leave the campfire, but do not attract attention if you want to live. Anyone I see trying to alert the guards will be killed without hesitation or remorse. Once you've left the camp center, each of you will need to make your way toward the perimeter gate. You need to be far away from the fire. Understood?"

Again, the youth nodded. Satisfied that his instructions would be followed, Veral let go of him and pushed him back toward his companions, disappearing into the shadows once more. The male gaped at him but then rushed forward and whispered to his companions. Each of them shifted their gaze around as if searching for any sign of Veral, and he smiled grimly to himself. Though they eyed their surroundings warily, they proceeded with caution as one by one they edged away from the fire.

Once he judged their distance sufficient, Veral grinned fiercely. He wouldn't need to get too close to the fire to get the job done; he would merely have to step far enough out in the light to get within throwing distance.

Sliding the bag of explosives off his shoulder, he gripped the bag in his left hand as he straightened to his full height and strode out among the humans. To his amusement, no one noticed his presence among them at first. They raved at all sides of him, their barely clad bodies writhing so monstrously that he smiled. He walked unseen among them like an incarnation of death until a human, larger and more heavily muscled than his companions, caught sight of him and froze. The alarm went up almost instantly, those nearest to him lurched forward in their zeal, but Veral dispatched them. Drawing his blade, he cut down those nearest to him, blood splattering over his armor as he rushed forward to the fire.

His systems locked on to his target.

The embedded circuitry in his joints fired, providing extra power as he spun the bag around and let it fly across the space. The lower gravity on the planet worked in his favor, sending the bag effortlessly toward its target. He spun around, his vibrissae whirling around him as he sprinted away from the fire. The humans tried to run, but they did not get far. He turned his head at the last minute to see the tote land in the largest fire. The fibers began to smoke immediately. Veral pressed his components to their maximum as he raced across the compound.

Moments later, the explosion rocked the compound. He saw the silhouettes of males up ahead of him freeze, highlighted as they were by the flash of light before he was momentarily blinded. Though he was thrown off his feet upon impact, he rolled and surged up again, running blind. He felt only the briefest impact of the soft, wet projectiles falling upon him in the aftermath, smelling of blood and flesh. He grimaced, knowing even without being able to see that human gore that had pelted him from the bodies caught close to the blast. Veral shook his head against the deafening ringing in his ears and the white light behind his eyes. As he ran, his senses returned. He was able to make out blurry shapes as his vision came into focus and sharpened.

At about that time, he was finally able to hear it. He heard the human screams of pain filling the air, some of them sounding less than human coming from warped chest cavities and twisted vocal cords.

His eyes searched through the dark before falling upon the shaky youths he'd sent out ahead, slowly and unsteadily beginning to rise to their feet. He noted that all were accounted for as they struggled forward again, noticeably spooked by the sound of the screams.

With his nanocybernetics flooding his system to repair the damage from the blast, Veral soon recovered. It took him little time to catch up with them. They stumbled as they ran, their faces pale from shock, though pinched with determination. The wails faded as they gained ground and as those caught in the fires fell. With a low growl, Veral pulled up by their side. They flinched at the sight of him, nearly falling, yet somehow keeping each other upright as they ran.

Veral's eyes homed in on the male he'd spoken to. "Move! You will find safety this way. Do not drop back unless you desire to remain here."

Though reeking of fear, all seven males ran faster at his threat, staying as close as they dared as he led them toward the compound gate. For their sake, he kept his pace slow enough to be reasonable for human ability but stopped short, fury flooding his veins at the sight that greeted him at the compound's gates.

erri groaned as she rose to her feet. Her ears were still ringing, but gradually she was able to hear the crying baby she'd offered to carry for a weary mom. Shushing the little boy as she bounced him, she watched the women assisting each other up from the ground. Everyone looked shell-shocked, their faces pale with dust and grit. They shook their heads and a few of them began to whimper. At the sound, the toddler in her arms began to wail, bringing his mother instantly to her side. Terri smiled in relief at the woman and handed the little one over as the other woman mouthed her thanks.

Coughing on the dust in the air, Terri inspected the women. "Is everyone okay? Becky?"

"Yeah, I think so," Becky grumbled. "I think I had the safest spot of all the ladies. This son of a bitch barely moved during the explosion. How about everyone else?" she shouted back.

Affirmations floated forward as women brushed themselves off and blinked their eyes. A few of the small children cried, but for the most part everyone seemed to be unhurt.

"Looks like Veral set off the dynamite. That had a bit more of a kick than I expected," Terri said. She brushed the sand from her hair and face and squinted ahead. The torches of the gate glowed just up ahead. She smiled with relief.

"All right, ladies, we're almost there. Is everyone ready to get the hell out of here?"

A tired murmur swept through the women, but they nodded their heads, and many wore smiles on their faces. Becky lifted a trembling hand and pointed to the gates.

"Let's get a move on, ladies," she croaked. Terri glanced at her in concern. The cloth covering the stump appeared to be fully saturated with blood now. That wasn't good. Becky fastened her with a hard look and shook her head. She didn't want the other women to worry. Terri pinched her lips together but reluctantly remained silent.

"Time to go," Terri agreed as she pushed her pack up higher on her shoulder. Once they were a safe distance from the gates, they would take a break and she would distribute supplies.

Everyone began to advance when a woman burst out screaming to the rear of the group. "A Reaper is coming! Hide!"

All the woman flew into a panic, a confusion of voices all crying out in unison. Terri pushed her way back through the women straining to hear the voice calling out to them.

"No. It's okay! Please wait for me. I'm not a Reaper!"

Terri froze in recognition, her eyes widening. "Everyone, it's okay. Calm down. It's Meg!"

The name was recognizable only to a small minority, a few of them twisting their lips in a knowing grimace of distaste. Terri frowned at them.

"Every one of you has had to do what you needed to do to survive. Meg made her choices and suffered for them."

A commotion erupted as one of the women shoved to the fore. Terri recognized her, the woman's fingers twisting around the small blanket that had been wrapped around her little girl. She'd refused to leave without it.

"Don't any of you bitches say nothin' bad about Meg," she said tearfully. "She wasn't like some of the other women in the camp.

She never did anything to hurt any of us and tried to deflect anything that Dale had planned. She brought me back my baby after those men hurt her. She didn't have to do that, and sure as hell none of you would have. You can pretend you're superior but not a one of you is better than her," she said to the few smirking women, effectively wiping the superior looks off their faces. Another woman came up behind her, wrapping her arms around the weeping woman as she shuddered and sobbed.

There was a stunned silence. Becky snorted, shattering the quiet. "Hell, I'll welcome her. It's not like I haven't seen plenty of the women in that shed spread their legs for the boys coming through, willingly or not. I don't shame anyone keeping herself alive."

Several ducked their heads in embarrassment while other women voiced their agreement with Becky.

"We women need to stick together," another one said, earning more mumbles of approval.

Meg stumbled over to her, barely visible in the low light from the nearby torches. Terri winced in sympathy at the dirty and bruised woman. Meg's dark hair was hanging in a tangled mass in her face as her body shivered with nerves. A wide smile stretched over her friend's face as she cried out.

"Holy fuck, Terri!"

Terri grinned and rushed forward to meet her friend. They embraced tightly and Terri laughed with relief.

"Meg, I am so happy to see you," she said as she hugged her friend close once more. "I was worried that you didn't get far enough away in time." She hesitated and looked around warily. "Dale?"

Meg shook her head with a watery smile. "Bastard tried to use me as a bargaining chip to save his own skin. Your *mate* took care of him—the whole mate thing I'm dying to hear about, by the way," she joked. Her shaky laughter turned into a sob as she clutched Terri tighter. "I've never been so scared."

"It's all right," Terri soothed. "We're going to get out of here and put this shit behind us. You are going to live in a safe place on the coast, get married and have a crap-ton of kids."

At the mention of children Meg's face crumpled and her shoulders shook with sobs. "I can't, Terri. I can't go through that again and lose my babies. I just... can't."

She stroked a hand over Meg's face, brushing her hair back. "Okay, well, no pressure on the kids part then. The point is you're going to have a fresh start."

Meg nodded her head and sniffled.

Her arm braced around her friend, Terri started forward once more. Her entire body ached from the blast, and exhaustion quickly began to wear at her. It seemed to take forever, but the torchlight slowly grew the closer they got. She smiled as they filed up to the gate at last.

"This is it!" she cried back to the other women. "Freedom."

She faced forward and staggered to a stop as a tall man stepped out from the other side of the gate. He was accompanied by a pair of males that looked like... Veral.

"My apologies, ladies, but I'm afraid I can't let you do that. I have struck a deal with these... gentlemen," he said smoothly, though the aliens looked at him balefully. He didn't appear to notice as he rambled on. "We've come to an agreement. It seems one of you lovely ladies managed to mate with their species. They've come to take said lady, and the rest of you, back to their world for observations of some kind."

"Marcus," Meg whispered. "What are you doing?"

"Becoming set for life. They delivered a significant amount of supplies and promised me transportation out of this dust heap just for handing you over. Quite profitable for me. Now, which of you is the lucky lady?"

He looked among them, his eyebrows raised. "No volunteers?"

"Enough of this," one of the males growled, his optic implant moving noticeably as his glowing iris turned and expanded. "We will just take them. Veral'monushava'skahalur will recognize his mate when he comes." He turned and glanced at his companion. "Deal with the betrayer."

Marcus's smile fell. "I'm sorry, what?" He looked from one to the other, his eyes widened as a blaster was pulled out and leveled at his face. The loud discharge from the weapon made Terri jump, her breath panting out of her in terror. Marcus's body twitched, his face nothing but a gaping hole, before he finally collapsed into the dirt at the feet of the Argurmas.

Holy shit!

The first male turned and looked upon them sternly, eyes steely. "I am Anakmasha'senat'amibdar, Lieutenant of the First Guard of the Imperial City of Argurumal. One of you has broken our laws, but in doing so may have opened an opportunity for a study of your genome if your codes are as compatible with ours as your mating indicates. You will have the honor of possibly strengthening Argurumal. Your presence is required." He paused. "Any female who comes forward will be… rewarded."

"Don't you dare, Christie," one of the women hissed.

"You heard it… We'll be rewarded! I want far away from this hellhole," Christie said. She craned her neck. "Hey! It's that one over there, the blonde holding up her dark-haired friend, Meg."

The Argurma rumbled as his head turned, his silver cybernetic eyes resting on her. A low growl rattled in his chest and his mandibles expanded, lips parting to draw in her taste and scent. There was a strange red flash in his pupil, and he nodded. "Confirmed. DNA presence of Argurma implanted embryo lifeform. You will come with us, female."

Terri shook her head in denial as she stumbled back, dragging Meg with her. The massive, dark hand shot forward, grabbing ahold of her before she was able to retreat more than a foot. He dragged her forward, removed a silver band from his belt, and snapped it open.

"Hey, what about my fucking reward?" Christie shouted.

Anak, as Terri mentally dubbed him, turned to his companion and gave him a meaningful look. The male moved over to her, pulling out an identical band that was snapped immediately around her neck.

"Your reward will be to become experimental breeder EB02 and join EB01 for testing of your codes. Zarnolmatek'inyafor'kashen lost his mate. He will have the honor of breeding you. You will enjoy considerable renown for your contribution." His head turned as he looked down at Terri. "Come, EB01." He was still staring down at her when he addressed Zarn in their own language. The other male smirked, throwing Christie over his shoulder with one arm as he pointed his blaster at the women huddled together. "All females will proceed in order without complaint. You will provide good genetic base material for our scientists to experiment with."

"Great. Going from the slave of one group of assholes to science experiment of another," Becky groused.

"And silence will be required," Anak snarled. He unholstered his blaster and pointed it at Terri. "Come, EB01," he repeated, his mandibles rattling in irritation.

Terri could see his vibrissae moving around him with aggression. Terri swallowed but her heart leaped just seconds later when Veral strode into the torchlight. He was smudged with gray dust and ash from the campfire, but she didn't think she'd ever seen a better sight. His eyes strayed to her to make sure she was okay before returning to narrow on Anak.

"Anak, release my mate, and these females under her protection."

The male chuffed without humor. "You are not one to make demands, Veral. You have been an outcast of our civilization too long—a reckless, malfunctioning system on the verge of destruction who has dared to flaunt our customs. At least your miserable life is worth something through the offspring you've seeded in this female. This new blood will be studied to see if there is anything that we can harvest to make our species stronger. Be honored that you were able to provide at least that."

Veral stepped forward again.

Anak cocked his head at him. "What are you going to do? Attack your own and bring dishonor upon yourself and your mother's house?"

"Of course not," Veral snapped, and Terri's heart sank.

Anak chuffed, "As I thought." He turned away to fasten the band around Terri's neck. She stared at her feet in disappointment. She didn't know what made her look up, but when she did, it was to see Veral soar through the air with his claws extended.

The male shouted as he attempted to shrug Veral off, but her mate climbed his way up until he was able to reach over Anak's shoulders, his claws digging in and rending through the scales and flesh over his neck and chest. Unlike a human, the warrior didn't go down right away. He twisted himself repeatedly as he choked on his blood. It was just enough of a distraction, however, that Veral's hand was able to slip down unnoticed to the blaster held tightly in Anak's hands.

The males fought and twisted, blood smearing between them as they battled each other over the blaster, fangs and claws flashing as they struck at each other. Terri heard a scream, but she couldn't tear her eyes away from the struggle in front of her. She willed Veral to win. She watched as her mate pulled back his clawed hand and swiped it in punishing blows over and over across Anak's face. The male spat out blood as he glared up at him.

"You are willingly dishonoring your mother's house. You truly are malfunctioning," Anak choked out.

"I am not. I honor my mother by honoring my mate. She is mine to protect!"

Finally, he twisted the weapon out of Anak's hand, his body lifting away from the male as he leveled the blaster at the male's exposed face and fired.

The blast sounded just as loud as before and made Terri's eyes water. She rushed over to her male with a shout, throwing herself against him. His arms caught her easily and pulled her tightly against his body, his mandibles purring to soothe them both. "Thank the gods," she whispered.

"Fuck. Umm, guys, where did the other baddie go with the dumbass chick?" Becky asked.

Veral snapped to attention, a snarl ripping out of him as he swung around, barely in time to evade the blaster shot. Pushing Terri to the ground, he rounded on the male, bringing his own blaster up. He fired twice, the lasers hitting the male in a vulnerable point in his armor between his chest plate and abdominal plates at point-blank range. Zarn stumbled back, blood pouring over his armor. Despite how grave his wound looked, Terri knew that his nanos were working to fix him.

She watched as her mate stalked right up to him, refusing to give his opponent even the slightest chance to mend. His tall, muscular body seemed almost a part of the shadows, his vibrissae trailing and snapping behind as he lifted his hand and swiped his blade, cutting through the tissue of his neck to saw right through his spinal cord. With a wet pop, the head separated from the body and Veral spat on the corpse before turning and repeating the process on the other. His task done, he kicked the heads away.

"These are not worthy trophies," he growled.

Without another word needing to be said, he turned and drew Terri into his arms. She leaned into him gratefully as his embrace tightened around her.

"Wow, that was something else." Becky whistled. "I guess this is a bad time to tell you I'm on the verge of passing out."

Terri immediately wiggled away, with only a marginal protest from her mate, and ran to the other woman's side. "Shit! You should have said something if you felt so bad," she chastised gently. Becky grinned up at her weakly.

"Like that was going to do me much good. Don't worry about me. I'm too damn mean and stubborn to die."

"You will not die, female," Veral broke in harshly. He looked at the blaster and turned a small dial on it. "I am changing the setting to one that will be efficient for cauterizing your wound." He hesitated and looked over at her. "It will hurt."

"I can handle it," she croaked.

"A lot," he clarified, with a trace of what appeared to be compassion on his face.

"She gets it, Veral," Terri hissed. "Don't freak her out."

He nodded his head quickly as he finished resetting the weapon. "Unwrap her leg, anastha." Terri complied and he held it out in front of him. He glanced at Becky once more. "Brace yourself."

Becky gripped the sides of the collector cart and gritted her teeth. The red ray of the blaster shot out, searing the end of the stump. A terrible smell of burning flesh filled the air. When Becky began to scream, Terri dove in to hold the woman in place until Veral finally turned off the beam. He frowned at his work.

"It is not surgically precise, but you will live without risk of infection."

Copious tears streamed down Becky's face, but she looked up at him with gratitude. "Thank you. Now—let's get the fuck out of this awful place. I've had more than enough of this screwed up desert."

"Man, that was crazy intense," a boy's voice said.

Terri turned her head in disbelief to see seven boys standing awkwardly off to the side. His eyes widened as he pointed to Veral.

"We're with him."

Turning to her mate, Terri lifted her eyebrows. "*You* brought those boys with you?'

His vibrissae snapped uncomfortably as his mandibles clicked. "They were being forcibly conscripted. I gave them the opportunity to escape, nothing more."

Another boy stepped forward, twisting the hem of his shirt nervously. "We swear we won't cause a problem…"

A loud shriek cut him off as a woman came barreling forward. "George Matthews! Is that you?"

"Oh, hi, Mom," he said with a sheepish smile. "I know you said not to come looking for you if you went missing, but… well, here I am."

The woman fell on her son, slapping the back of his head before grabbing him against her and holding him tight. "You foolish, crazy boy!"

Veral watched them with a peculiar look on his face — something like longing if Terri wasn't mistaken. Gently, she nudged him.

"We'd better get going. I'm sure everyone would like to reunite with their loved ones."

Nodding, he turned reluctantly, his grip not once breaking from Terri's hand, and headed out into the city, the small band of women and children following after them. No one was more surprised than Terri when Christie limped toward them from wherever the Argurma had dropped her and followed sedately at a distance behind them. She still couldn't believe the woman sold her up the river. She shot her a glare over her shoulder as she leaned into her mate.

23

*V*eral scowled at the young males as they lingered a short distance from the safety of his shelter. He did not trust them in his place of rest or being so close to Terri. At least not without what Terri called ground rules. He liked the term. They followed the rules, or he would personally flatten them into the ground. They were mature, no longer small offspring, and would be accountable for their actions.

He stalked around them and the youths shrank away, though they wore brave smiles of expectation. He narrowed his eyes at them, wondering how seriously they were taking him. "Make no mistake, you are here only at my indulgence. You will not threaten any females while in my territory. You will not touch the one called Terri on the threat of great pain and possible dismemberment of your favorite appendage. Indicate that you understand these instructions."

All the males hastily jerked their heads in the affirmative, their eyes wide. Veral grunted approvingly.

"You will conduct yourselves as honorable warriors in training. You will hunt and gather food and learn to spar to protect your clan... familial unit. I shall not tolerate any complaints. As honorable warriors, you will not coddle the females. You will respect them, but you are not there to serve at their bidding. Courting of any kind is on your time as long as it doesn't cause any disruptions until the time that I deposit you on the coast. I shall squash disruption without hesitation. Does this compute?"

The males rushed to nod at his words.

Veral turned away, his mandibles clicking as he made his way through the alleys toward his abode, leaving them to follow. He was well aware of their presence just behind him as they followed a short distance away. He did not care if they feared him, though he doubted that they feared him as much as they should. He was satisfied as long as there was some measure of fear. A healthy fear of him was wise on their part and would keep them from acting inappropriately.

Krono rushed to greet Veral as he returned to the domicile. He could hear the inventive human cursing behind him as those following him got a good look at his dorashnal. He patted Krono's neck and glanced up as Terri came into view from the doorway.

"You males! Go inside and mind what I said. Krono will protect the females if you threaten them in any way!"

One by one, they filed past him into the dilapidated building, each of them eyeing the dorashnal with trepidation. Krono's tails were held out stiff from his body as he watched them before turning to lope after them into the building. Terri watched after them, the corners of her lips quirking, before she turned her gaze to him, her eyes softening in a way that she seemed to reserve for him, much to his pleasure. "Did you scare them too much?"

Veral chuffed. "Only marginally for behavioral correction."

Her teeth flashed, and she laughed. "That's okay. I think it'll be a good offset from all your admirers in there. The women we rescued have been asking after you for the last hour."

He made a sound of disgust, his vibrissae fluttering around him anxiously. "I do not care for their attention."

"I couldn't tell," she said, a playful edge to her tone. Sarcasm, she called it. She ran a hand through her yellow hair thoughtfully. "The caravan was heading west to the coast, but the other women are of a mind to go as well. Do you have enough room in your ship to carry everyone? They'll have to wait until we're done salvaging, but I'm sure they'd appreciate the shorter, safer trip."

He inclined his head in agreement. "It would be logical. There is plenty of space with the cargo hold empty. It will not be comfortable, but it will be a short flight." He hesitated, his eyes flicking over her. "However, we do not need to wait for the salvage to end. I confess that I recognize their needs outweigh my own. I have decided to cease salvage on this planet for the time being... It is not optimal, at least not until something can be arranged with the Council for their protection as per intergalactic law for salvaging planets occupied by sentient species. There are other targets in this system that may have a better yield."

Terri's brows winged up as she leaned in. "Oh yeah? Sounds like it might be an adventure."

Veral trilled in the affirmative, his mandibles purring with pleasure as her breasts brushed against him as she fitted herself closely against him.

"So how many rooms does this exploration vessel have on it?"

He frowned thoughtfully. "One dining hall, the main command, the armory, and five cabins. What is your purpose for inquiry, my mate?"

"Well, according to that asshole Anak, your seed has taken hold with an embryo. I mean, we have time—three years from what you say," she laughed, "but I figure that gives me plenty of time to decorate a nursery for our little one."

Veral turned her in his arms, his hands skimming her belly. "We will have plenty of time for safe adventures before our offspring comes."

His mate scowled at him and punched him in the shoulder just below the horn. She cursed and shook her hand out from the force of the impact. "Fuck, you're built like a tank. Look, mister, you need to take a page out of your own rule book—I won't be coddled."

"I said nothing of coddling," he stated mildly. "Our adventures will just be scheduled to prevent any risk to you or our offspring."

"Not much of an adventure without some risk," she muttered. "You said yourself that our baby won't even grow noticeably until the third year. That means we have time for a *real* adventure."

He growled, his mandibles clicking. His mate sighed and rolled her eyes. To his surprise, she reached up, grabbed some of the lower trailing vibrissae that always seemed to seek her out, and dragged his head down to her. Veral was caught off-guard as she pulled him down to press her mouth against his. The sensation was completely alien. Argurma didn't do any such thing, but it was so pleasurable he couldn't imagine why not except for the disadvantages of both members of a mated pair possessing mandibles.

Sweeping her up in his arms, Veral carried her through the domicile, ignoring the eyes of those watching them as he made his way to their room. Depositing her on the nest of fabrics, he smiled down at her, his fingers touching his lips.

"I am curious to see what else these can do."

Leisurely he stripped her of her armor as he made his way down her body, caressing her exposed, delicate skin with his lips and tongue. His mate sighed as he explored, the sounds and scents of her arousal growing as he played along her flesh. When he reached her sex and brushed against it with both of his tongues, her body quivered and arched into him as she shouted his name, her voice raw with demand.

Curious, he spent much time between her thighs, sliding his tongues around the little bead of flesh that gave her so much pleasure before dipping into the sweet cavern that flooded his mouth with so many unique flavors that he couldn't get enough of feasting on it. He lost count of how many times she cried out when he tasted and sucked at her flesh. He had no idea how many more times she screamed out his name when in a fit of desperation, his civix straining madly, Veral had slipped out of his own armor to join their bodies together, his sex buried deep within her own, seeking bliss.

The next morning was the dawn of a new life together as they led the humans into the desert to his starship. The very people who had seemed so broken and exhausted yesterday seemed to find strength on that day. They smiled and spoke to each other of the things they looked forward to as they faced another future and left the desert behind them. Some of the newer additions were still nervous around Krono but anxiety seemed to be low and there was a certain calm expectancy. All except for Becky, who, with the prosthetic he fashioned for her with the replicator, was striding through his ship to "get a good look at everything while she could," by her own admission.

Although it taxed his patience, he allowed it because it made his mate smile. Besides, even though Becky was far too inquisitive, she was not disruptive in her explorations, which earned her some favor with him. Still, he was eager to deposit all the females in their new home so that he could be alone with his mate for a while. His ship was crowded and the noise made his ears and head hurt.

He watched eagerly through the viewscreen as the ship moved quickly over the desert until barren land started turning green and the sea rose up, crashing against the shore. He glanced at his mate seated at his side wearing one of the beautiful loose robes he'd fabricated for her. He liked seeing her there. The command center of his ship seemed empty before when he thought back on it. She turned her head and smiled patiently at him as he adjusted his receivers until he found a signal that he expected was coming from the sanctuary that the females had spoken of. Following it up the coast, he flew for some time at an easy pace so that Terri could enjoy the view.

When they finally arrived at the source of the signal, Veral's heart dropped with dread. Amid a green valley, a white city rose up from where it was tucked behind a small mountain that, according to his calculations, protected it from the storms that brewed over the seas. Everywhere around it, green things grew. It seemed to be the most ideal place for humans to thrive—clean with plentiful food and water.

As they approached, he was able to see a number of humans spilling out into the courtyard as they watched his ship descend with expressions of awe and fear on their faces. Once, he might have enjoyed that, but now he just wanted to be on his way. As he looked at the beauty of the area, part of him feared that his mate would abandon him to remain.

He set his ship down and opened the portals wide, releasing the females from the hold.

24

*T*erri paced in the gardens, a flower in her hand. Everything was so beautiful, as she'd once imagined it might be, but she felt restless. The people were perfectly welcoming... to every human who arrived, anyway.

They were reserved around Veral, making it abundantly clear that they did not care for his presence. She knew they were afraid of him, but they also claimed that his very presence disturbed the peace and tranquility of their city. In true Veral fashion, her mate had scoffed at the claim, earning him few favors. He had been absent more often, leaving her to explore the city alone. That disturbed her not only because she missed his company terribly, but because many of the men took every occasion to court her despite her vehement insistence that she was already mated.

Thank goodness for Becky. If she ever thought Josie was a force of nature, the woman had nothing on her daughter. Becky had run off all of Terri's suitors when her own tactics didn't work. After having to endure it for the fourth time that day, Terri was annoyed with them and her absent mate.

Snarling a curse under her breath, Terri threw the flower down and stomped out of the garden, heading directly for the ship, where she knew Veral was holed up. Dreaming up every insult she could fling at her male, she entered the ship and headed straight for the command station. Krono looked up at her from where he lay as she peeled through the doorway. She glanced down at him in passing only to collide with the person she was seeking in a rain of flowers.

Falling on her ass, she coughed and sneezed as pollen scattered over her. Brushing flower petals off her, she looked over and met the eyes of her mate. His vibrissae were flattened to his head as he stared down at the tempest of flowers, not meeting her eyes.

What was going on with him?

Leaning forward, she plucked a few scattered petals off his nose and cheeks, her lips curving into a smile. "These must have been very beautiful flowers," she said softly.

"I searched for the best I could find, but it was more difficult than I believed. I tried to calculate what dimension would make the most pleasing flower but failed to find those that perfectly fit my expectations. I know human customs involve a demonstration of flower-giving to show their affections. My databases state that is because flowers represent sexual organs, but it is strange as it seems more expedient to just show one's own sex. Regardless, I wished to adhere to something you would recognize and enjoy. I wanted to find the most favorable flowers to demonstrate the height of my feelings."

She chuckled and eased forward so that her body rested against his. "That's incredibly sweet, and I love that you think of me that way, but Veral, sometimes something is beautiful even with its imperfections. I'm not perfect, nor do I expect a gift to be perfect. It's important because it comes from you. I don't even need flowers to show it. Love is what's important." She pillowed her head on his chest and looked up at him as his arms closed instinctively around her. "Do you love me, Veral?"

"The word love is one that occurs frequently in the downloads I retrieved from your satellite. There is nothing like it in the Argurma language. My programming would suggest such emotions would be due to malfunctions in my system, but I know that is not true. I find that this love matches close to my feeling for you, though it doesn't express the depth of my emotion enough. I have never felt for another, anastha, and yet for you, I feel everything."

"That sure sounds like love to me," she whispered. "I love you too, Veral."

He gave her a sidelong look. "You would not prefer to stay among the humans and find a more... *suitable*," he growled out, "mate in this place?"

Terri snorted. "Find a guy... here? I would die from boredom. We haven't even been here a full day and already I'm bored. Honestly, Veral, I can't believe you would even think that. I don't wish to be parted from my mate. I love *you* and would miss your crotchety attitude way too much. Besides, I think I still owe you a debt."

His glowing, blue eyes narrowed on her, his vibrissae shuddering as a smile kicked up the corners of his lips. "You do have an unresolved debt," he agreed. "You are a good partner, plus I would... enjoy your company. You may also find the chance to visit many planets rewarding and of interest."

A slow smile stretched over her lips. "No need to sell it to me. You had me at 'I love you.' I'll follow you anywhere after those three little words."

He huffed. "It would have helped if someone had told me that it was that simple. I've been trying for hours to find the best way to convince you to stay."

"The flowers were a good start," she agreed, her grin widening.

He stepped forward and dragged the back of his knuckles over her jaw, obviously enjoying the way her eyes dilated at his touch. She enjoyed watching his own narrow pupils expanding with desire at the simple contact. "I look forward to spending a great many years proving it to you. I can think of none other I wish to be with, bond or no," he murmured.

"All right," she breathed. "I'm all yours."

Veral drew her into his arms, his vibrissae surrounding her as they leaned into each other. Dropping his head, he nudged her with his nose before tilting his head to seize her lips in a kiss. Terri groaned with pleasure, happily getting lost in the sensation. Gradually, she became aware of the ship moving, rising up from the ground as it prepared to enter orbit. She giggled and surrendered completely to his ravishment.

A blinking light distracted them and eventually caused him to pull away from her.

"What's that?" she asked.

He frowned. "An exterior receiver. Someone is trying to hail us from outside of the ship." With a flick of his fingers, he turned the viewscreen to the source of the disruption. Two female humans jumped up and down, waving their arms below the ship. Terri laughed as she recognized her friends.

"Terri, don't forget about us!" Meg shouted. "I love you!"

"And be sure to take advantage of all the time you have ahead of you getting plenty of alien dick!" Becky yelled happily. "I would totally be in your place right now if I could get a good one... one that's available, anyway." She laughed.

The women blew kisses to her and Terri clutched her hand over her heart. Veral nuzzled her cheek.

"It is time, anastha."

She nodded her head, a wide smile spreading over her face as the ship accelerated up into the atmosphere, leaving the broken remains of Earth far behind them.

EPILOGUE

Three months later

TERRI HOPPED OFF THE MEDICAL PLATFORM — REALLY MORE LIKE med-bed — as Veral studied the results. Ever since they left Earth, he'd insisted on weekly monitoring of the embryo. Given the satisfied look on his face, she knew that the results were still positive. Terri only disliked the regular exams because it reminded her of how her pregnancy would be. Even at three months, her baby was a teeny tiny lifeform developing very slowly in her womb, so there wasn't much to get excited about for some time yet.

In the meantime, she preferred to keep her hands busy.

His eyes slid over to her. "Scans show you are in good health and the embryo is on target for development. The nano signature is already strong. You need to eat more of the axna fruit that we picked up at the space station, however, to boost your vitamin intake."

Terri groaned and made a face. The fruit native to Argurumal was disgusting. It was green with an almost tear-drop shape and covered with spines. She could live with that. Veral was always careful to peel the fruit and segment it for her. What she disliked though was the dry, leathery texture and nutty, meaty flavor that she couldn't bring herself to enjoy.

Her mate caught her look of revulsion and rumbled in disapproval. She gave him an innocent smile in return. "I'll try to eat more," she amended solemnly. "So where are we headed to next?"

Aside from plenty of alone time with Veral and enjoying a very active sex life, Terri never ceased to be amazed by space travel. She'd come to learn that their ship did more than just salvage, though that was the bulk of their income. It was also supported by regular retrievals for odd clients. They had already delivered a heavy bride-price in jewels and escorted a princess of Nizzirn to her new husband, after which they traveled to the arctic planet of Waivul to retrieve a large shipment of native furs to deliver to a trader on the Xenxinexa Space Station.

Every day was an adventure, though she suspected that Veral was picking through the job offers for those which had minimal actual adventure. They had yet to do another salvage job, but when he illustrated for her how such operations usually went, it sounded dull enough that she didn't mind.

Although his caution frustrated her at times, such as the way he'd kept her on a short leash throughout the space station and had forbidden her from exploring large portions of it, she couldn't be too mad. Everything was so new to her that it took little to entertain her. If Veral tended to be broodier and more possessive over her and their unborn offspring, it didn't often show—well, except for that incident with the Manvi. It had attempted to touch her and then had two of its tentacles ripped off and shoved so far down its throat that it had to be taken the emergency medical bay. The Manvi had been fine—the species apparently breathed through gills—but the males on the space station gave them a wide berth after that.

Her mate's eyes gleamed at her, not at all fooled by her tactic. "After you eat your fruit, we will be heading to the Megnax system. There is wreckage on the planet that we are being paid well to salvage and return all valuables to the royal house of Grez'na."

Terri leaned forward, eyes wide with excitement. "Was the ship brought down by pirates?"

Veral frowned. "I did not think to ask. That may change the situation..."

"What pirates hang around wreckage?" she scoffed. "Pirates sink ships, raid, and move on with whatever treasure they find. Sometimes burying it and setting elaborate traps. You really should read *Treasure Island*. It's already in your database," she remarked.

Thanks to a common implant that nearly everyone in the Federation had, Veral had been able to upload basic reading comprehension skills for her language, as well as a few common trade languages. She'd once looked at the tattered remains of books longingly, wondering what worlds were held within their pages. She had far-off memories of her grandmother reading to her and wondered what she had been missing all this time. As soon as she received the download, Terri spent hours reading files of Earth books that he had downloaded, soaking them in voraciously, book after book.

Her mate chuffed. "If you say so, anastha. I will perhaps take that into consideration. Regardless, I will scout the area thoroughly for any sign of pirates before we go anywhere near the planet."

He turned and headed toward the command center, Terri hot on his heels.

"Perhaps it is a *cursed* treasure," she said with glee.

Her mate chuffed and nudged her with his forearm. Terri wrapped her arms around the appendage and hugged it to her chest. But when she stepped away to release him, he stopped her. His vibrissae twined through her hair and he pulled her up against his body, resting his jaw and mandibles affectionately on top of her head. She grinned up at him and snuggled into his embrace. She couldn't wait to begin yet another new adventure with her mate. Sometimes it almost didn't feel real.

On the nights when she dreamed of Earth, she would wake up in a cold sweat, certain that meeting Veral had all been a dream and that she was still foraging among the ruins, eating out of cans that she was fortunate enough to find, starving as she slowly died. On those nights, Veral's arms would instinctively react to the tension in her body, tightening around her so that she knew she was lying in the circle of her mate's arms.

It was all it took to dispel those nightmares.

She knew that someday her memories of the broken and dying planet would eventually fade—though from time to time she would think of Josie, Meg, and Becky, hoping they were well—and then she would be free to fully enjoy the long life ahead of her at his side.

She had a lifetime of adventures waiting for her.

Author's Note

I hope you enjoyed Terri and Veral and their story. *Broken Earth* started out as a submission for a Dystopian Anthology that failed to be accepted into the final round of submission selection. I fell in love with the story so much that I decided to expand it into a full-length novel. While the book itself is complete, depending on how well it is received, I do plan on doing two more books for Terri and Veral, and maybe even other books in the same world for Becky and Meg. Each book introduced will be a complete novel without a "to be continued" and able to be read independently if desired.

Fans who've been around for a while know that I love the Predator, and some features inspired my Argurma species. I call them my mix between dark elf and Predator in design with a bit of something extra thrown in. I also wanted them to be a cybernetic species as I love cyborg books. So this was my first foray into the Cyborg subgenre within Science Fiction Romance.

When it comes to *Broken Earth*, many fans who had the opportunity to receive the original short story for free during the "Cyborg Monday" event in December 2019 will notice differences in the plot. I had the option of picking up where the short story left off and expanding it further, or expanding and making small changes to the plot of the short story. I chose to do the latter so the ending had to be tweaked quite a bit. I do hope however that everyone finds the changes enjoyable!

Thank you so much for joining me. I truly loved writing this book. Keep an eye out for Book 2: Pirate's Gold introduced in novella form in the They Come from Beyond Anthology June 2020.

S.J. Sanders

OTHER WORKS BY S.J. SANDERS

The Mate Index
First Contact
The VaDorok
Hearts of Indesh (Valentine Novella)
The Edoka's Destiny
The Vori's Mate
Eliza's Miracle (Novella)
A Kiss on Kaidava
The Vori's Secret
A Mate for Oigr (Halloween Novella)
Heart of the Agraak
A Gift for Medif

Monsterly Yours
The Orc Wife
The Troll Bride
The Accidental Werewolf's Mate

Sci-Fi Fairytales
Red: A Dystopian World Alien Romance

Ragoru Beginnings Romance
White: Emala's Story

Dark Spirits
Havoc of Souls
The Mirror (also part of Mischief Matchmakers)

Shadowed Dreams Erotica
The Lantern
Serpent of the Abyss

ABOUT THE AUTHOR

S.J. Sanders is a writer of Science Fiction and Fantasy Romance. With a love of all things alien and monster she is fascinated with concepts of far off worlds, as well as the lore and legends of various cultures. When not writing, she loves reading, sculpting, painting and travel (especially to exotic destinations). Although born and raised in Alaska, she currently as a resident of Florida with her family, her maine coon, Bella, and pet bearded dragon, Lex.

Readers can follow her on Facebook https://www.facebook.com/authorsjsanders
   Or join her Facebook group S.J. Sanders Unusual Playhouse
   https://www.facebook.com/groups/361374411254067/

Newsletter: https://mailchi.mp/7144ec4ca0e4/sjsandersromance
   Website: https://sjsandersromance.wordpress.com/

Printed in Great Britain
by Amazon

87277570R00123